RUN
FOR THE
HILLS

*'It doesn't matter if the paws are black or white, so long as they
can catch a mouse.'*
Old Sage Brush

TOM McCAUGHREN lives in Dublin and has worked as a journalist and as a broadcaster for RTE. He has always been interested in wildlife, an interest that prompted him to write the fox series, *Run with the Wind, Run to Earth, Run Swift, Run Free, Run to the Ark, Run to the Wild Wood, Run for Cover* and now *Run for the Hills*.

His books have been widely translated and have won many awards including: the Reading Association of Ireland Book Award 1985; the Irish Book Awards Medal 1987; the White Ravens Selection 1988 (International Youth Library Munich); The Young Persons' Books of the Decade Award 1980-1990 (Irish Children's Book Trust); and the Oscar Wilde Society's Literary Recognition Award 1992.

RUN
FOR THE
HILLS

THE MULTI-AWARD-WINNING SERIES

ILLUSTRATIONS BY BEX ATKINSON

TOM McCAUGHREN

THE O'BRIEN PRESS
DUBLIN

This edition first published 2016 by The O'Brien Press Ltd,
12 Terenure Road East, Rathgar, Dublin 6, D06 HD27, Ireland.
Tel: +353 1 4923333; Fax: +353 1 4922777
E-mail: books@obrien.ie
Website: www.obrien.ie

ISBN: 978-1-84717-876-3

6 5 4 3 2 1
20 19 18 17 16

Printed and bound by Norhaven Paperback A/S, Denmark.
The paper in this book is produced using pulp from managed forests

Published in:

DUBLIN

UNESCO
City of Literature

For my grandchildren,
Caoimhe, Tom, Annabelle and Senan

CONTENTS

ONE

THE GREAT WHITE FOX

All the foxes who lived in Glensinna knew about Sionnach, the Great White Fox. But they had never seen him. Some thought that on one occasion they might have, but it was only a fleeting thought and one that had passed like the melting snow. When they were cubs their mothers had told them the story as they whiled away the time in the darkness of their earth. Even before the cubs could understand what was being said, their mothers told it. Secure in the warmth of their mothers' embrace, the story was whispered in their tiny ears.

Once upon a time, she had told them, the fox god Vulpes had reshaped the hills and formed a valley especially for them. It was a valley where they could survive when others who lived elsewhere might not, a place where the Great White

Fox would look after them in times of great danger.

Perhaps man had once seen a white fox there. Why else should he have called it in Gaelic, Gleann an tSionnaigh Bháin, which means the Valley of the White Fox? If he had, he had long forgotten it, as he now called it Glensinna.

The foxes that lived in the valley called it the Land of Sinna. But they had not forgotten why. They knew the story only too well. And those who thought they might even have seen the Great White Fox were not young foxes given to telling tall tales. They were grown-ups.

It was winter time when it happened. The snow was falling and for a moment they thought they had discovered who the white fox was. But then, as they reflected on what they had seen, they had to admit that it could have been their imagination. For the fox who seemed to be white was, after all, one of their own, his frail back covered by a mantle of snow. Because of their uncertainty, it was a story they kept to themselves. Then there was a most unexpected occurrence.

One day, as one of these foxes hunted for food, she came face to face with what seemed to be the creature of her mother's stories. Like most foxes, she herself had a white tip on her tail. But this one was completely white, from its face to the tip of its tail – and it wasn't snowing!

TWO

COATS OF MANY COLOURS

The beech leaves had turned brown, the birch leaves yellow and the sycamores a mixture of both. On other trees, nature had added a splash of gold and crimson to the leaves and in doing so turned the countryside into a rich kaleidoscope of colour. At the end of a long row of beeches, the wind plucked a leaf from a branch and played with it as it made its downwards spiral. It landed on the nose of an old fox who was dozing in the leaf litter beneath. He shook his head to dislodge it and raised his whiskered head. The edge in the wind and the looseness of the leaf told him much. Autumn was well on its way and winter would soon come riding on that wind –

winter and the many dangers it would bring.

Easing himself to his feet, the old fox turned and made his way through the hedge into the next field. He could feel the remains of plastic that had shielded the seeds of maize in spring and was aware of the rooks and pigeons that were now feeding among the rows of stubble. The birds took no notice of him, nor did he take any notice of them. His earth lay in the next corner where four hedges met. The entrance was concealed by huge mounds of hedging that was intertwined with all sorts of weeds and creepers. The crows and the pigeons that perched on the ash tree above knew the earth was there but they paid no heed to it. An old fox posed no danger to them. He, on the other hand, would pay much heed to them when they returned to the tree with their craws full. For their eyes were his. They could see from their vantage point what he could not see. They would be long gone before danger arrived and so would he.

Danger, however, was soon to take a form that it had not taken before.

Farther along the side of the valley, a vixen was lying in the back garden of a big house. It was a split-level garden and she was in the upper part looking down into a room where a woman came and went. It was still daylight but the lights were on in the room and the vixen could see that on a rectangular table in the centre were the remains of a bird, a chicken perhaps, or a pheasant, she couldn't be sure. She knew that the carcase of the bird would soon be thrown out. So did the two dogs that waited outside the back door. She had watched the dogs devour the leftovers before and was determined that this time she would have some of them for herself. The dogs, she had noted, were old and fat from being over-fed. They waddled around waiting for food and, she reckoned, would be incapable of pursuit.

A short time later the kitchen door opened and a man threw the remains of the bird into the yard. The dogs got up and ambled towards them, only to change their minds when the man threw smaller pieces farther out. As the dogs made their way over to those, the fox sped down to the door, grabbed the skeleton of the bird and ran back up the embankment. The dogs were so busy competing with one another for the smaller pieces of food that they didn't even see what had happened. However, the man did and ran back in.

Hearing the man shouting, the fox paused at the top of the embankment and looked back. The dogs, she could see, were running around barking but, thankfully, not posing any danger. She turned to go when, to her surprise, she found herself looking into the eyes of a white fox. It showed no fear but just stood there looking at her. Somehow time seemed to stand still, the red fox staring at the white, the white one staring at the red. Stories that the red fox had been told as a cub were swirling through her mind – stories about a great white fox who would always be there for them in times of trouble. She was rooted to the spot, mesmerised by what she was seeing, unable to comprehend it.

More shouting snapped her out of her trance and turning around, she saw two men emerging from the house with guns. She had seen men with guns before. It was at this time of year that they went to the meadows to shoot ducks or pheasants or anything else they might find. She herself had once suffered at the hands of the shooters and she immediately realised the danger she was in. Racing to the boundary hedge where she had made her way in, she turned and looked back. To her shock she saw that the white fox still hadn't moved. It was if it thought it couldn't be harmed.

Fortunately, the two men seemed so startled by the sight of the white fox that they too stood there for a moment not knowing what to do. Dropping the bird, the red fox streaked back across the lawn and, circling slightly, knocked the white fox over. As the two foxes raced away, the men opened fire and ran forward to see if they had scored a hit. In their hurry to get to the top of the embankment, however, one of them slipped on fallen leaves and fell back. His gun went off and the screams that followed told him that he had shot his friend instead.

On the other side of the hedge, the white fox stopped again. Dropping the bird once more, the red fox rushed back to tell the other fox to put a spurt on. There was screaming coming from the garden and looking through, she saw to her surprise that one of the men had dropped his gun. He was holding his hips with his hands and hopping around and it was he who was doing the screaming. Blood was seeping through his hands and, whatever about the white fox, the other fox realised that the man had been shot. From the way he was screaming she guessed he was in great pain, and once more she was reminded of the time that a man like that had shot her in the hip. She also recalled how a fox with a black tip on his tail had come to her aid and saved her by picking the pellets out of her skin with his teeth.

'Come on,' she whispered to the white fox. 'We'd better get out of here.' Picking up the skeleton of the bird, she raced on through the fields. Now and then she stopped to see if the white fox was following. It was, but it didn't seem to be in any hurry. In fact, it didn't seem to know what it was doing. Perhaps, she thought, it wasn't afraid of the shooters. And if it was the white fox of her dreams, why should it be afraid? It was a creature that couldn't be harmed. If the shooters came, it would simply disappear, like the dreams themselves. However, there was only one way she herself could disappear, and that was to run. With one last glance back at the white fox, she flung herself through the next hedge and, taking a circuitous route to confuse any dog that might follow, made her way up along a row of beech trees and across to a small disused quarry where she had her den.

'A white fox?' Her mate laughed. 'You must have been

eating toadstools. Was it the ones that grow on fallen trees?'

'I haven't been eating any toadstools,' she replied frostily. 'In fact, the only food I found was what you're eating now. And I haven't had any of it yet.'

'Sorry.' Her mate pulled back a bit so that she could have some of the bones. 'So, tell me all about this white fox. Where did you see it?'

The two of them were lying in a den beneath an over-hanging rock in the bottom of the quarry which was covered with a thick growth of bushes and briars. As they munched the skeletal remains of the bird, the vixen related everything she had seen.

'And where's this white fox now,' her mate asked.

'I don't know. I couldn't get it to run. It didn't seem to be afraid.'

Like all foxes who lived in the valley, her mate had also been told stories of the Great White Fox. Like the others he believed that it did exist, but only in foxlore, not a real fox like themselves. Now his vixen was telling him that she had actually come face to face with the white fox. But how could that be? Belief in something that might or might not exist was one thing. To see it in the flesh, on the ground was something else. It would mean it was a creature like them-selves, not one that floated across the hills and valleys, forever watching over them. So what had his vixen seen? He had never known her to exaggerate. He had heard others tell tall stories of their hunting exploits, but not her.

Making his way up through the undergrowth, he emerged onto the rim of the quarry. There he sniffed the wind. It carried no hint of man or dog, but he got the scent of fox. He turned around to trace the scent in the wind and to his surprise saw three foxes sitting on a small rise not far away. They were in plain sight and seemed quite unafraid. Realising that they could draw danger down upon his mate and himself, he rushed over to them. As he drew closer he realised to his utter amazement that they were quite unlike any foxes he had ever seen. One was pure white. Another was blue, but its underfur was grey. The third had a black face and legs, but the fur on its body was silver.

'Who are you?' he asked. 'What are you doing here?'

When they didn't reply, he told them, 'You'll get yourselves killed, sitting out here in the open like this.' Once again they didn't answer. Anxiously he looked around. Seeing no sign of man or dog, he told the three, 'You'd better hide or we'll all be killed. Follow me.' He made to return to the quarry but, on glancing back, saw that they still hadn't moved. 'Hurry!' he barked at them. 'Follow me.'

When he reached the rim of the quarry, he was glad to see that the three strange foxes had decided to follow him. Reluctantly, it seemed, they came over to him and after some urging, followed him down through the undergrowth to the quarry bottom. There they sat back on their haunches and waited, but for what?

As the red vixen emerged from the den, she was equally startled at the sight that met her. However, she managed to say to her mate, 'I told you I saw a white fox.'

'And what about the other ones?'

'I didn't see the other ones. If I had, you surely wouldn't have believed me.'

The two of them lay down at the mouth of the den and wondered what to do. For a while none of them spoke.

'What's your name?' asked the female red fox. 'When there was no reply, she told them, 'I'm Vickey. This is my mate, Black Tip.'

'Where are you from?' Black Tip asked.

None of the three strange foxes replied, nor did they reply to any other questions. They just sat there and stared, a blank expression on their faces.

'What are we going to do with them?' asked Black Tip.

Vickey shook her head. 'I don't know.' She paused. 'Maybe we should ask Old Sage Brush. He might know.'

Black Tip nodded. 'Okay. You wait here. They seem to be harmless enough. I'll go and find him.'

When Black Tip entered the field of corn stubble, he could see that some crows and pigeons were feeding while others had retreated to the ash tree where the four hedges met. He was pleased to see them, not because he wished to catch any of them but because he knew that when they were there, man was not. The last thing he wanted to do was to put the old fox in danger.

'A white fox!' Old Sage Brush laughed. 'And a blue one!'

That's right,' Black Tip assured him. 'The other one is silver, but its ears and legs are black. So is its tail.'

It was a long time since Old Sage Brush had seen a fox of any colour, as he was blind. Black Tip had often acted as his eyes and now he realised that he must see through the eyes of his friend again. 'It's difficult to imagine,' he said. 'Tell me more.'

Black Tip told him how the white fox had followed Vickey from the garden of the big house and how two more had joined it near the quarry. 'They look like us in some ways,' he explained, 'yet in other ways they're different. Apart from their colour, their fur is very fluffy. And they move slowly, cautiously, almost as if they're afraid of us. But they're definitely foxes.'

'Did they say where they came from?'

'That's another thing. They haven't said anything. They just sit looking at us.'

Old Sage Brush nodded. 'It must be getting very crowded down there.'

'It is.'

'Okay then. If they won't talk to us, maybe it's time we talked to them.'

The three oddly-coloured foxes were still sitting in the quarry looking at Vickey when the others arrived.

'They still haven't said anything,' she told them.

Black Tip joined her and lay down at the mouth of their den, looking at them.

Old Sage Brush sniffed to see if the scent of the visitors would give him a clue. 'It's an odd scent,' he remarked. 'Heavily laden with the scent of man – and mink, if I'm not mistaken.' He moved closer but the three foxes immediately jumped back.

'They're very nervous,' Vickey told him. 'Maybe it's because we are a different colour.'

'To me a fox is a fox whatever its colour,' said Old Sage Brush. He lay down as if to assure the three foxes that he meant them no harm and after a few moments asked them, 'Where are you from?'

When they didn't reply, he said, 'You understand what we are saying, don't you?'

The three glanced at one another and shifted a little uncomfortably as if afraid to confide in him. Then the white fox eased itself down and spoke for the first time. 'Yes, we do understand what you are saying. But we come from a different world. Your world is so strange. We have never been in it before.'

'Does that mean you come from that other world?' asked Black Tip. 'The one we go to when we leave this one?'

'Don't be silly,' said Vickey. 'You know that once we cross over there we can't come back.'

'I know that,' replied Black Tip. 'But foxlore tells us there is a white fox who can.'

'The only one who can is Sionnach,' the Old Sage Brush reminded him. 'He is the Great White Fox, the one who watches over the Land of Sinna and the one who will help us if ever the need arises. This white fox, I believe, is in need of help itself — and, if I'm not mistaken, is a vixen. So also the one you say is the colour of the sky, and the one you say is the colour of night and of day.' He paused, adding, 'Close your eyes and you will see them as I do. They're just foxes.'

'You friend speaks as if he can't see us,' said the white fox.

'He can't,' Black Tip confirmed. 'Man has seen to that.'

'It's true,' said the old fox. 'I am blind, but that doesn't mean I'm deaf. Furthermore, I can see you in my mind's eye, and sometimes that eye can see farther than the two we have in the front of our head. Now, what do you mean when you say you come from a different world?

The blue fox and the silver one eased themselves down beside the white one and between them they told of a world in which, it appeared to the red foxes, there was no blue sky and no green grass, no rivers or meadows, no hedgerows or birds, no farmsteads, no hens, no ducks, no badgers. Only mink — white mink. A world devoid of life and colour, except that of their own. A world in which they had no need to hunt. A world in which man was their friend — or so it seemed.

THREE

A STRANGE NEW WORLD

The wind was getting stronger now. It blew across the fields and in along the hedgerows, searching out more leaves that were ready to fall. Occasionally it whistled through the briars on the rim of the quarry, but it didn't disturb those who lay below.

'This is all so strange,' whispered the white fox. 'We've been told all about it, but this is the first time we've seen it.'

'Seen what?' asked Black Tip.

'This world of yours.'

'And your world?' urged Vickey gently. 'Tell us more. '

The white fox licked one of her front paws. 'What more can we say? Ours was a world of wire. You have a den. We had a cage.'

'And were you all in the same cage?' asked Black Tip.

'No, we were in separate cages, except at mating time. Just like the others. But we were caged beside each other so we became friends.'

'You mean there were more foxes there?' asked Vickey.

'Yes. You see, we were kept in a long shed and there were many foxes in it of many colours.'

'There were no sides in the shed,' said the silver fox, 'and we could see there were other sheds with cages of foxes. Mink too – white mink.'

'But where did man capture you and all these other coloured foxes?' asked Old Sage Brush. 'When I could see, I never came across a fox who wasn't the same colour as myself. Nor a white mink, and I travelled far and wide.'

'We were not captured by man,' explained the silver fox. 'We never lived in your world, only the cages we were born in.'

'But you say you've been told all about our world,' said the old fox. 'If you were born and bred in a cage, who would tell you such a thing?'

'We were not all born and bred in a cage,' the white fox told him. 'Sometimes we saw a man coming into the yard and when he carried a sack over his shoulder we knew that a red fox was about to cross over from your world into ours.'

'A red fox,' muttered Black Tip.

The blue fox nodded. 'Usually only males and females of certain colours were allowed to mate. But the red fox would also be allowed to mate with some of us and then we would have foxes of quite a different colour.

'This man who brought the red fox,' asked Black Tip. 'What was he like?'

The white fox shrugged. 'Man is man. They're all the same.'

'I mean, what did he look like?'

'He was tall and wore something on his head...'

'The one thing I noticed,' said the blue fox, 'was the paw.'

'What paw?' asked Black Tip.

'The one he wore around his neck.'

'The trapper!' exclaimed Vickey.

'You know him?' asked the white fox.

'Only too well,' said Old Sage Brush. 'He has killed many foxes in this valley.'

'He sets traps for us,' Vickey explained. 'I don't know which are the worst, the choking hedge-traps or the snapping jaws.'

'Black Tip,' said the old fox. 'I think you should go up to the blackthorns and get Hop-along.'

A short time later Black Tip returned with two other foxes, one of which the strangers could see, had only three legs.

'Hop-along, She-la, this is...' Vickey stopped. 'Sorry, I didn't get your names.'

'We have no names,' the white fox told her.

'Oh. Then I must think of some.'

Vickey, they were amused to learn, had given names to some of her friends. Her mate she had called Black Tip because he had a black tip on his tail instead of a white one. Another she had called Fang because he had strong teeth.

'So what will you call me?' asked the white fox.

'Because your fur is white as snow, I will call you Snow-flake. And you, with your fur as blue as the flowers of the wood, I will call you Bluebell.'

'And what about me?' the third one asked her.

'Your hair is tipped with silver, like the frost that settles on the grass, but when the wind blows it, it is black. So, what will we call you?'

'White Tip?' suggested Black Tip

Vickey smiled. 'I don't think so. We may not have a white tip on our fur, but we all have a white tip on our tail – except you of course.'

'What then?' the silver fox asked her.

'I don't know. We could call you Silver. But then, you're not really silver, are you? What do you think, Sage Brush?'

'In the darkness of my mind,' said the old fox,' it is not the morning frost that has settled on her fur I see but the shades of night that lie beneath. Why don't we call her Nightshade?'

Vickey nodded approvingly. 'All right then, Nightshade it is.'

'Thank you,' said the silver fox. 'Somehow it feels nice to have a name. In the other world we had none.'

'What about your own name?' asked Snowflake. 'What does it mean?'

Vickey smiled. 'My mother thought it would suit me because I was a vixen.'

'And am I right in thinking you are all vixens?' asked the old fox.

'Yes,' Snowflake told him. 'We were kept for breeding – otherwise we would not be here.'

'Because we'd be dead,' added Bluebell.

'What's this all about?' asked Hop-along. 'Where did they come from?'

Vickey told Hop-along and She-la how she had met Snowflake and what she and her friends had told them about the strange world they had come from. Then, addressing Snowflake she added, 'Tell them about the man who sometimes came with a red fox.'

'You mean a dead one?' asked Hop-along.

'No, a live one,' said Snowflake. 'It was put into one of our cages and one of us was allowed to mate with it.'

'I don't mean that,' Vickey said. 'Bluebell, tell him what the man was wearing around his neck.'

'He wore a paw around his neck. I think it was the paw of a fox, a red fox.'

'It was the paw of a red fox,' Hop-along told them. 'I know. It was my paw.'

'My mate caught his leg in one of the man's traps,' She-la

explained. 'He had to chew off his paw to get out of it.'

Bluebell cringed. 'That was a very brave thing to do.'

'I had no option,' said Hop-along. 'It was either that or die.'

Black Tip shook his head. 'I still don't understand. If you were born and bred in the cages, how did you learn to talk like us?'

'We were not always caged,' Nightshade told him. 'Or at least our ancestors weren't. They were wild once just like you. Their stories were passed down to us from one generation to another. Their way of talking too.'

'Tell us more about your life in this other world,' said Old Sage Brush. 'How could you eat if you couldn't hunt?

'You have soft grass to walk on and a den to lie in,' said Snowflake. 'We had only wire to walk on and wire to lie on. The cage was our den. It was the den of every fox that lived there. The cages were in rows in a long shed. The shed had a roof but, thankfully no sides. And so our world was the space in which we could turn and the space we could see beyond.'

'But I ask you again,' said Old Sage Brush. 'How could you eat if you could not hunt?'

'Man fed us,' replied Snowflake.

'Man?' asked Hop-along incredulously.

'That's right,' said Nightshade. 'He would come chugging along in his machine, spewing food into our cages.'

In his mind's eye, Old Sage Brush thought of man's

machines cutting meadow grass and spewing it into a high-sided trailer. It could hardly have been as big as that, he thought, but said nothing. It was difficult to imagine something he had never seen.

'He had to feed us,' added Bluebell, 'for we couldn't get out to hunt – not that we know how to hunt, or what to hunt. We have heard you hunt rabbits and raid man's cages for his chickens. But we have never seen rabbits or chickens.'

Black Tip shook his head in amazement. 'And what was in this food that you got?'

'The captive red foxes told us it tasted like rabbit, chicken and fish,' said Nightshade.

She-la turned up her nose. 'Ugh. Fish is for mink. They live in the river.'

'We have never seen a river,' said Snowflake. 'But the red foxes told us about it.'

'It must have been very difficult for you,' Vickey said. 'I mean living in such cramped conditions.'

Snowflade nodded. 'It was. But at least we were able to live our lives and mate – unlike many of our cubs.'

'Why, what happened to them?' asked the old fox.

'When they were born it was our best time, and their best time,' Snowflake recalled. 'We lived in a box and it was so much more comfortable than the wire. The cubs were full of life – just like we were when we were young – but it didn't last long. When they were weaned they were taken away and we were returned to our cages. Next time we saw them they weren't quite fully grown, but big enough to be put in a cage like ours. They were ready to run and jump and stretch their legs at that stage, but suddenly the cage had become their world. All they could do was turn and pace, turn and pace. Sometimes we were able to talk to them, but it was no use. They just spent their short lives pacing their cages the way we paced ours. It was all very distressing – for us and for them.'

'What do you mean their short lives?' asked Hop-along.

'Because they *were* short,' added Snowflake. 'At least for most of them.'

'As soon as they were fully grown,' said Bluebell, 'this man would come. He was fatter than the others and when we saw him we were in great fear, not only for the young foxes, but for ourselves.'

'How come?' asked Vickey.

'Because he was the one who decided which of us would go and which of us would stay. Dog or vixen, it made no difference. The ones he pointed to were taken from their cages and we never saw them again. The others were kept for breeding.'

'But you were already being kept for breeding,' said She-la. 'So you were safe, weren't you?'

'Yes,' Bluebell replied, 'we were safe all right. But only so long as we were the colour he wanted.'

'And those that were taken?' asked Hop-along. 'What happened to them?'

'We had no way of knowing,' said Nightshade. 'But we knew it wasn't good, for none of them ever came back.'

'Then one day a captive red fox was put into one of the cages,' said Snowflake. 'He couldn't settle down and we could see he was very upset. We thought it was because he was confined to the cage, but it was more than that. He kept pacing around his cage and showed signs of great stress, something that wouldn't usually happen until a fox had been in a cage for some time. At first he didn't speak to us. Then he told us he had seen something so terrible he couldn't bring himself to talk about it. Gradually we convinced him it might help if he told us. Eventually he agreed to do so, and when he did it was as if our world had come crashing in on us.'

Bluebell lowered her head. 'We were sorry we asked. It was so terrible we all became very upset.'

Bluebell began to sob and Vickey turned to Snowflake. 'What did he tell you?' she asked gently

'He told us that when the trapper took him out of the sack, he saw the skeletons of many foxes in the yard – a huge pile of them.'

'But that's not all,' said Bluebell. 'In a shed he got a glimpse of many fox furs – rows and rows of them. It was only then we realised why we were being kept in the cages.'

'They were keeping you for your fur!' said Vickey.

'But why?' asked Snowflake.

'For the same reason he wanted our fur,' said Old Sage Brush. 'Vickey, you tell them.'

'At one stage the trapper killed many foxes in this valley,' Vickey recalled. 'Him and others. We didn't know why, but it got to the stage there were few of us left. Then Old Sage Brush took us on a great journey so that we might learn how to be cunning again.'

'Cunning enough to outwit the trappers,' added Black Tip.

'And it was on that journey,' continued Vickey, 'that we learned why man was killing so many of us. We knew it was not for food as we sometimes saw the trapper skin the bodies and throw them away.'

'It was from a little fox in Man's Place that we learned why,' said Black Tip. 'His name was …'

'Scavenger,' said Vickey, taking up the story again. 'Little Scavenger. He didn't have great fur of his own. But he took us to a place where we saw that man had turned the coats of the foxes he had killed into coats for his own kind.'

'Coats!' exclaimed Snowflake. 'But man has his own coat to keep him warm. Why should he want ours?'

Vickey shook her head. 'I don't know. It was a sight I shall never forget. It made me shiver. Of course, we were free to go – you weren't. It must have been awful for you.'

Bluebell nodded. 'Each time the fat man came to take some of us away, we cringed, for we never knew who would be next. We felt as if we wanted to die – but not that way.'

'Then something wonderful happened,' said Nightshade.

'What?' asked She-la.

'One night,' said Snowflake, 'the yard outside our cages became very bright, almost white.'

'The Great White Fox!' whispered Black Tip.

Vickey gave her mate a look that told him to be quiet.

'Before we knew it,' Snowflake continued, 'dark figures were running around the sheds, shouting. At first we were afraid they were coming for us. And they were, but not to kill us. To our great surprise they opened the cages to let us out. But we were afraid to leave. We had never been outside our cages before and we didn't know what to do. Then we saw the white mink streaming across the yard and out through a hole in the fence. I think Nightshade was the first to move and the rest of us followed. Suddenly we were free.'

'Maybe it was this great white fox you speak of,' said Bluebell. 'What did you say his name was?'

'Sionnach,' said Vickey.

'Maybe he did cross from your world into ours. Maybe he threw the protective light on us. I don't know. But, as Snowflake says, suddenly we were free.'

'But free to do what?' recalled Nightshade. 'When daylight came we found ourselves in your world and we didn't know what to do.'

'Strange,' mused Old Sage Brush. And he thought to himself, 'Sionnach may have thrown a protective light over the captive foxes, but if he did he must have forgotten about the rest of us.' Getting to his feet, he said, 'We must call a meeting.'

'You mean at Beech Paw?' asked Black Tip.

'Yes. Hop-along, you and I will stay here to make sure our new friends don't stray. The rest of you travel far and wide as you have done before in time of crisis. The young foxes have gone, but tell those who have stayed behind that we must talk.'

'When?' asked Vickey.

'There is no time to waste. They must see the colour of these foxes themselves if they are to understand. So I would suggest the time between darkness and dawn when they can come and go as they please and man is not yet up and about.

★ ★ ★

In yet another world, the world of man, the release of the foxes and mink was told in a very different way.

An animal rights group had discovered an illegal fur farm being operated by a man in a wooded valley far from prying eyes. Animal fur had come back into fashion, and he was sending pelts abroad at a time of growing demand in the industry – a demand reflected in the modelling of exotic furs on the catwalks of London and New York.

Working in secret and without a licence, he was free to

cage his animals and harvest their furs without visits from inspectors and the standards of care imposed on licensed farms. Such supervision he regarded as a hindrance to production and he was anxious to avoid it, especially now that the demand for his mink and fox furs were on the increase. He was also anxious to avoid the attentions of animal rights groups who were opposed to all fur farming, whether licensed or not.

Somehow, one of these groups had found his farm, but in freeing the animals from their cages they had unwittingly put the red foxes that lived in Glensinna in the utmost danger.

FOUR

BACK TO BEECH PAW

Within the circle of beech trees known to those who lived in the Land of Sinna as Beech Paw, sat a circle of red foxes many of whom had travelled from miles around, and within their circle sat three foxes of a different colour. One was white as snow, another was black with a sprinkling of frost, while the third was as blue as the bells of the wood.

When the red foxes who had answered the call got over their astonishment, one of them said, 'Who are they? And what are they doing here?'

Between them, Vickey and Black Tip told them what had happened.

'And what are we supposed to do about it?' asked another of the red foxes.

'That's why we've asked you to come here,' said Old Sage

Brush. 'We have to talk about it.'

'What is there to talk about?' asked yet another red fox.

'We must decide what to do about them,' replied the old fox. 'As captive foxes they have not learned how to hunt.'

'Give them a rabbit,' suggested a fox sitting at the back of the circle. 'One each and let them be on their way.'

The old fox lay down and stroked his grey whiskers. 'Give a cub a rabbit and you will feed it for a day. Show it how to hunt and you will feed it for a life-time.'

'But they are not cubs,' said another fox.

'No,' said the old fox, 'but they might as well be.'

'I thought we were only to meet here at Beech Paw in time of crisis,' said a fox who was lingering at the back.

'But it is a time of crisis,' the old fox replied. 'As Vickey and Black Tip have told you, there were many captive foxes in the cages, foxes of many colours.'

'And many mink,' Vickey told them. 'White by all accounts.'

'And whatever about us,' said Black Tip, 'we fear that man may come in great numbers to get them.'

'The trapper will be after them,' said She-la, speaking for the first time. 'Hop-along and I live in fear of him. And we fear there will be others.'

'Shooters too,' added Vickey

She-la nodded. 'And they'll shoot anything that moves whatever its colour.'

Some of the other red foxes nodded. They were aware of

the fact that Vickey and She-la had once been injured by the shooters and knew it was a miracle that they had survived.

Hop-along, who was lying beside his mate She-la, shifted uncomfortably, but said nothing.

'We felt we must warn you,' Old Sage Brush continued, 'and decide what to do.'

'We don't have time to show them how to hunt,' said one of the red foxes.

'Then we must leave them to their fate,' said another.

'We can't abandon them just because they are not red like us,' said Vickey.

Old Sage Brush agreed. 'Vickey is right. The Great White Fox wouldn't look kindly upon us if we failed to care for others just because they're a different colour.'

'What would we do?' asked Black Tip, 'if he ceased to watch over us because we are not white like him?'

'Furthermore,' Vickey said, 'it appears from what they have told us that the Great White Fox may have helped them to get out of their cages.'

The other red foxes were in awe of this and whispered among themselves, uncertain now what to do.

The fox who had been lingering at the back turned to go. 'It's obvious they can't stay here,' he said. 'If what you say is true, the shooters and the trappers will soon be upon us. We must all be on our way or we too will be in danger.'

Old Sage Brush nodded. 'Surely I know you. You sound

like a strong fox and one that may have shared my thoughts in the past.'

'It's Fang,' exclaimed Vickey. 'Our old friend, Fang!'

Hop-along got up and hobbled forward. Fang had been a great strength to them in the past and somehow his presence now seemed to infuse his mind, if not his three remaining legs, with something akin to added strength. Or was it just a feeling of greater comfort?

Black Tip, who had once fought with Fang over Vickey, said to him, 'Don't leave. Help us decide what to do.'

Others, however, were already leaving. They had decided that, whatever about the Great White Fox, there was only one thing to do – go their own way and look after themselves.

Old Sage Brush got up. 'Fang is right. We cannot stay either. If man comes he will kill many of us, regardless of our colour. I am too old to out-run him and he has left Hop-along too lame. As for the captive foxes, they don't know how to run.'

'That means we must all get as far away from here as possible,' said Black Tip. 'But the question is where?'

'There is only one place we can go,' the old fox told him. 'As you know, the food in our territories can only feed so many of us. That is why we stay away from man but close enough to prey upon his farms. However, I am told that in a land beyond where the eye can see there is a place where there are fewer farms – and fewer foxes. Perhaps it is a place where our friends might find a home.'

Fang, who had come closer, asked, 'And where is that?'

'In the land close to the hills – the Hills of the Long Low Cloud.'

'I have never heard of such hills,' said Fang, 'and I have hunted far and wide.'

'Nor I,' said Black Tip, 'but they sound as if they are a long way away.'

'You're not suggesting that we take them there?' asked Vickey.

'Why not?' said the old fox.

'But you are…'

'Old?'

'No …' Vickey looked for the right words so as not to offend him. 'I was going to say you are not as young as you used to be. It would be a very difficult journey for you.'

'And for us,' said She-la.

Hop-along nodded. 'I doubt if I can go.'

'I know it will be difficult for you,' the old fox told him. 'But you can't stay. However, if we go now we can get a head start and perhaps you and I may not have to run so fast.'

'So, who have we?' asked Vickey. She looked around now to find that all the other red foxes had slipped away. All, that is, except one. 'Fang,' she said. 'Will you come with us?'

Fang lowered his head. 'I don't know. I, ah, have other plans.'

Vickey nodded. Mating time wasn't far away now and she reckoned he would be looking for a nice vixen with whom to have a family. 'I understand,' she said. 'But…' She looked at the three coloured foxes, 'Our friends have crossed over from their world to ours. They have no mates to help them, so we must help them.'

'They find themselves in a world in which they must fend for themselves,' said Old Sage Brush, 'but they cannot hunt. It is a world in which they should be afraid, but they know not what to fear; a world in which they must be cunning, but they see no reason to be; a world in which they are free to chose a mate, but they don't how; a world in which they can live like us, if we show them how.'

'We must teach them all the things we take for granted,' added Vickey.

'But you haven't time to show them,' said Fang.

'No,' said the old fox as Fang turned to go, 'not now, but we can show them along the way – if we hurry.' He turned to the others. 'Daylight will soon be upon us. It's time to go.'

During all this time, Snowflake, Bluebell and Nightshade said nothing, for they understood little. So when the number of red foxes was reduced to five and the five decided to go they tagged along, happy in their ignorance of the new world and unaware of the dangers they faced. Had they been aware of these dangers and the extent to which the loss of sight and a leg handicapped two of their protectors, they might have had second thoughts. As it was they followed the five, or was it six?

Black Tip led the way. As always he would be the eyes of Old Sage Brush. Vickey trotted behind the old fox, ready as always to be his inspiration when things got tough. Behind her hobbled Hop-along, weak in body but strong in spirit and as always supported by his mate, She-la. Behind them came the three coloured foxes blindly following the one who led and could not see; a fox who was weak in body but very wise and whose frailty would now get the strength of another. For a sixth red fox caught up with them and took his place beside Old Sage Brush. Fang, as always, would be there to be his strength. So it was that this small group now left the Land of Sinna and headed for the Hills of The Long Low Cloud.

★ ★ ★

Had shooters seen the small group of foxes leaving Beech Paw they could have wiped them out with a few shots. Fortunately, it was their custom to fix their eyes on the colours of the pheasant or the mallard as they took flight, rather than on their tracks. And now that a new breed of foxes had been let loose upon Glensinna, it was their colour rather than their tracks that they looked for.

The trapper, on the other hand, always had his eyes fixed firmly on the ground, and the tracks told him many things.

Most of the red foxes, he could see, had scattered and gone to earth leaving the coloured ones to the shooters. However, a few had left the valley. Usually, foxes were solitary animals, except at mating time, but these ones he noted, had not scattered. For some strange reason they were travelling in a small group. Furthermore, they seemed to be going in a fairly straight line, which was also very unusual for foxes.

The trapper's experienced eye also told him one other thing: the paw prints included several that were somewhat distorted, a sure sign that they had been made by foxes that had once walked on wire. The presence of coloured foxes, he knew, would soon attract trappers as well as shooters. When that happened, the valley which had long been his territory and his alone would no longer be his. But with luck, the coloured foxes that had left would hang in his shed along with those of the reds.

Unaware that their departure from Beech Paw had been noted, Old Sage Brush and his group travelled as far as they dared in daylight. Now and then they could hear shots in the distance, but shots can carry far in the cold winter air and where exactly they were coming from was impossible to tell. Nevertheless, it made them feel apprehensive and at the bidding of the old fox, Black Tip went ahead to look for a place where they could take refuge until nightfall.

When Black Tip returned, he reported that he had found an empty badger sett.

'Good work,' said the old fox. 'But you're sure it's no longer in use?'

'Certain. Grass and weeds grow at the entrance.'

Old Sage Brush nodded. Badgers, he knew, were very fussy about their setts. They kept their bedding dry and weren't ones to let grass grow under their paws. He also knew that badgers dug many tunnels in their setts and chambers for their young.

'Very good,' he added. 'There should be plenty of room there for all of us.'

And so there was.

Old Sage Brush was tired and sought out a small side chamber where he could rest. She-la found another where she could tend to Hop-along. Fang lay down near the entrance, his long black ears twitching to every sound, but there was no rest for him. Now and then he walked back through the main chamber where Black Tip and Vickey were keeping an eye on the foxes from the fur farm.

'Where is he going?' asked Snowflake.

'Badgers have very powerful claws,' Vickey told her. 'They dig deep and they dig well. We came in by the main entrance where they pushed out all the soil, but they also have more discreet entrances, or should I say exits, up at the back. Fang is just checking them to make sure we are not taken by surprise.'

'You mean, by badgers?' asked Nightshade.

Vickey laughed. 'No. By man.'

'We have never seen a badger,' said Bluebell. 'What is it like?'

'Well,' Vickey told her, 'it's black and with white stripes. Or is it white with black stripes. I could never tell.'

Black Tip smiled. 'A bit like you Nightshade. I mean, are you silver on black, or black on silver?'

Nightshade looked back at her fur. 'I don't know. I never thought about it.'

'So what are we waiting for here?' asked Snowflake.

'We're waiting for darkness to fall,' Black Tip told her.

'Why?'

'Because it's safer. You see, man hunts by day. We do too, of course, but we prefer to hunt by night when he's not around.'

'Maybe man cannot see as well in the dark as we can,' said Vickey.

'But how do you know where you are going?' asked Bluebell.

'We have our ways,' Vickey told her. 'And if we are going on a long journey like this, we have the Great Running Fox to guide us. When darkness comes, we'll show you.'

'That and much more,' Black Tip assured them.

As the red foxes talked, the three newcomers to their world dozed off. Having spent their lives in a cage, they were not accustomed to running and were tired. Black Tip smiled at Vickey and curling up beside one another, they closed their eyes too.

It seemed to them and the others asleep in the sett that they had only closed their eyes when Fang roused them to tell them darkness had fallen. By now the moon had come up and the stars were clear to be seen. It wasn't a frosty night but the air was cold and the breeze carried a variety of scents.

Old Sage Brush raised his nose and sniffed. 'A good night for hunting,' he observed. 'Black Tip and Fang, perhaps you might see what you can find. We must introduce our three friends to something better than what man spewed into their cages.'

When the two dog foxes had gone, the old fox said, 'Vickey, She-la – now might be a good time to tell them more about our world, and show them a little of that other world, which if I'm not mistaken, now twinkles above them.'

The old fox, of course, couldn't see the great canopy of the night sky. He couldn't see the full moon that was shining down upon them, or the myriad of stars in the Milky Way. But he sensed the kind of night it was and guessed they were up there to be seen by those who, unlike him were able to see. He turned and went back into the sett, adding, 'Hop-along and I have need of more sleep than the rest of you.'

Thankful for the opportunity, Hop-along hobbled after him. A journey like this did not come any more easily to him than to a fox who could not see – or, for that matter, a fox that had lived in a cage.

FIVE

THE FIELD OF THISTLES

It was with great wonder that the three foxes from the fur farm gazed up at the night sky, for they had never seen it before. Their only sky had been the dark roof of the shed in which they were confined. Beyond its edge they might have seen a star twinkling dimly in the distance, maybe even two. But they couldn't have imagined that above it was another roof that curved from one side of the world to the other and glittered with more stars than they could count. Some stars, they could see, were brighter than the others. Then their eyes came to rest on the moon.

'What is that?' asked Snowflake.

'It has the face of ... of man,' said Nightshade.

'And he seems to be smiling at us,' added Bluebell.

'That's the wide eye of gloomglow,' Vickey told them.

'You may think it resembles the face of man,' She-la said, 'but we think it is more like the eye of the fox. It's the same colour and gives us that nice half-light that we call gloomglow.'

The other three foxes now looked into the eyes of the two red foxes. In the stressful conditions in which they had been caged, the only thing they had seen in the eyes of their fellow captives was fear – fear of the time when man would come and take them or their cubs away. Now they found themselves looking into eyes that were round and yellow like their own but with no trace of fear. And when they looked up at the moon, which seemed to be smiling at them, they could see why the others called it the wide eye of gloomglow with such affection.

'Gloomglow is a nice time to hunt,' said Vickey.

'But how do you find your way?' asked Nightshade.

Vickey smiled. 'The wide eye of gloomglow gives us enough light, but it is the Great Running Fox in the Sky that shows us the way. See, up there. It is just coming down to touch our world. Then it will take off again, up and away on its own travels.'

'When it touches our world, we mark the spot well,' She-la explained. 'By doing so we can come and go as we please – even travel great distances – without losing our way.'

'But how do you mark it?' asked Bluebell. 'All I can see of your land is shadows.'

Vickey smiled. 'We have many secrets, and that is one of them. Don't worry. We will show you how.'

What the foxes were now looking at was the formation of stars man calls the Plough; the same one by which mariners of old found the North Star to guide them across the seas. The foxes, however, knew nothing of ploughs and boats. What they saw in this particular group of stars was the figure of a running fox, the last three stars forming its tail. And now as they gazed at them, She-la spotted the flickers of shooting stars. 'Look!' she exclaimed. 'There and there. Those are the spirits of foxes that have gone to the after-life.'

'We don't always see them,' said Vickey. 'But tonight they've come out to play.'

'And there's another one,' added She-la. 'We can only get a glimpse of their tails but we know they are happy.'

'And what's the difference between the Great Running Fox in the Sky and the Great White Fox?' asked Snowflake.

'The Great Running Fox is there for all to see,' Vickey explained. 'It comes down at night to guide us on our way. The Great White Fox we cannot see, but we believe it is always with us, that it has crossed over from that other world to watch over us and help us in time of trouble.'

'We have learned many things since we met you,' said Snowflake, 'and we have heard many names. You have even given us names. But you haven't told us where Old Sage Brush got his.'

'Old Sage Brush is the elder fox of our world,' Vickey explained. 'His name means wise fox and his word is widely respected. As we journey on you would do well to listen carefully to everything he says.'

The foxes from the fur farm said they would. However, they would find that some of those who respected the old fox most would begin to doubt the wisdom of some of the things he said.

A short time later, Fang came back from his hunting trip and they were glad to see he was carrying a rabbit. He told them it had been sitting out in the gloomglow and he had caught it off guard. They were all hungry, but the red foxes were aware that their three friends had been reared on a mishmash of food served up by man. So they stood aside and watched with great amusement as the three of them figured out how to dissect the rabbit and for the first time in their lives crunched the bones of rabbit caught in the wild.

Vickey and She-la were wondering what Black Tip would bring, when another creature came crashing through the undergrowth towards them. Startled, they bolted for the mouth of the badger sett. Then, fearing it might be a badger returning to reclaim its sett, they stopped and looked back. The other three foxes were still sitting where they were, unaware that they might be in danger.

Fang ran forward, ready to face the badger, if that's what it was. He knew he couldn't fight it, but was ready to distract it long enough for the others to get away. Seeing that it was another fox he stopped, and feeling greatly relieved told the others, 'No need to panic. It's only Ratwiddle.'

'Who's Ratwiddle?' asked Bluebell.

Ratwiddle came close to where they were, but didn't join them. Nor did he look at them. Instead, he sat back on his hind legs and started scratching himself. All the while his neck was craned up and around as he looked at the night sky.

'Ratwiddle's a friend of ours,' She-la explained.

'Why doesn't he speak?' asked Snowflake.

'And why does he keep looking up?' asked Nightshade. 'Is he looking for guidance?'

Vickey laughed. 'Far from it! He always looks up like that, whether he's sitting or running.'

'Why?' asked Snowflake.

'He's forever hunting for rats down at the lake, not far from where we first met you,' said She-la. 'We think they gave him some kind of sickness.'

'And fleas!' added Vickey. 'So if you want my advice, you'll keep well away from him.'

'If he doesn't look up for guidance,' said Nightshade, 'and he doesn't look down. How does he find his way?'

'The sickness seems to have addled his brain,' She-la told her. 'But in some strange way, for he can see better than any of us.'

'He can even see things before we see them,' said Vickey.

'Things that haven't even happened.'

Vickey edged as close to him as she dared. 'Ratwiddle,' she whispered. 'What do you see up there? Tell us so that we might know what dangers we face.'

Ratwiddle stopped scratching and, speaking as if he was drawing inspiration from afar, told her, 'In the darkness of my mind I see many things.'

'What do you see?' she asked gently, but as usual Ratwiddle didn't elaborate.

Frustrated, Vickey returned to the others and Nightshade went over and lay down beside Ratwiddle. When she came back, she told them, 'He says man will fear the fox.'

'I didn't hear him say that,' said Vickey.

'He also said the fox will hunt the man.'

'What a strange thing to say,' Snowflake remarked.

'And what a strange way to say it,' added Bluebell. 'It doesn't make sense.'

'What he says never makes sense,' Vickey told them, 'until it's too late.' She got up and went over to Ratwiddle again. 'What do you mean, man will fear the fox?'

However, Ratwiddle got up and dashed off into the darkness in a way that suggested he had no idea where he was going but had no fear for himself.

Vickey lay down beside Nightshade again. 'Are you sure he said what you said he said – you know, that man would fear the fox and the fox would hunt the man?'

Nightshade nodded. 'That's what he told me.'

Between them, Vickey and She-la told Nightsade and her friends more about Ratwiddle and how, in the past, his strange predictions had always come true.

A short time later, Black Tip returned with a pheasant. It provided even less food than the rabbit. There was very little to go around and Old Sage Brush announced that they would have to hunt by day in order to get something more substantial.

The words of Ratwiddle, relayed by Vickey, seemed to give the old fox food for thought and as the others talked among themselves, he lay on his own for a long time mulling over what their strange friend had said.

Hunger kept most of them awake during the night and when daylight came, Old Sage Brush sent Fang and Black Tip out again to forage for food. Something more substantial, he reminded them. But what?

It was Fang who first came across the geese. He heard them squawking long before he located them in a field beside a farmstead. There were a lot of thistles in the field which obscured his view, so he retreated to a low hill covered with gorse, where he could observe the geese unnoticed. As he watched them waddling around at the bottom of the field, he tried to remember when he had last seen geese at a farm. Even farmyard ducks were a rare sight. There was, he could see, a wide gap in the hedge nearest the farmyard where the geese could come and go as they pleased. He hadn't heard them during his last outing and guessed that the farmer took them in at night. Now they were sifting mud in a dip in the field that the rain had left quite wet.

The top part of the field was completely covered in this-tles and Fang reckoned they would enable him to get half-way down without being seen. However, flocks of gold-finches were feeding on the thistle tops, and the slightest noise would make them take flight. That would alert the geese. They would squawk even louder and if the farmer heard them he would know something was wrong.

As Fang wondered what to do, Black Tip joined him. He too had heard the geese, and agreed that one of them would be much more substantial than a pheasant. The problem was how to get close enough to take one. After discussing the possibilities and the problems, they decided to report back to Old Sage Brush.

It was a long time since the old fox had tasted goose, and when Fang and Black Tip told him all they had seen, he nodded. 'One of them would do nicely, and there would be enough for all of us. But you are quite right. Geese are always alert to danger and their squawking is usually heard by the farmer long before we can get near them.' He stroked his grey whiskers as he thought about the problem. 'Unless, of course, we can get them to come to us…'

'How can we get them to do that?' asked Fang.

'As I have told you before, if all else fails we must use our cunning. Hop-along. Are you there?'

Hop-along who was lying in one of the smaller tunnels with She-la, got up and hobbled over to the old fox.

'Somehow,' continued Old Sage Brush, 'I imagine that a fox like you would have more chance of fooling the geese.'

'You mean because I have only three legs?' asked Hop-along.

The old fox nodded. 'I think so.'

'But geese are not stupid,' Hop-along protested. 'And if there is a gander there it could be even more dangerous.'

'We saw no gander,' Fang sought to assure him.

'I am not saying the geese are stupid,' the old fox continued, 'but like all creatures they are curious, otherwise they would not find food in the mud. Now, here's what I want you to do.'

When Old Sage Brush had outlined his plan, Hop-along said, 'But I can't hope to hobble through the thistles without making a noise. And even if I did catch a goose, I wouldn't be able to drag it back.'

'She-la will go with you,' the old fox said. 'Black Tip and Fang will be nearby in case you need any help. They can watch from the hill and show our friends what it means to be cunning.'

Sensing from Hop-along's silence that he still wasn't happy about it, Old Sage Brush told him, 'If the hawk can fly through the branches of a tree without touching a leaf, surely a fox can pick its way through a field of thistles without making a sound.'

'The hawk has eyes second to none,' Hop-along responded.

'Better than the eyes of a fox? – I doubt it.'

'But the hawk has wings, we have not.'

'That may be,' added the old fox, 'but the hawk has only two legs. You have three.'

Hop-along could not really follow the logic of this. It sounded like a piece of nonsense. At the same time he knew the old fox was trying to goad him into going, while assuring him he could do it. 'All right,' he said at last, 'I'll try.'

'Good. And She-la – you'll go with him?'

She-la didn't like the idea any more than her mate, but she just said, 'Of course.'

'All right then. The two of you must exercise the greatest caution. The Field of Thistles will be a great challenge to you, but we must show our friends that hunting is a matter of stealth, not strength.'

The Field of Thistles, as the old fox called it, was partly covered in what man calls spear thistles, a sturdy weed with prickly stems and spear-like leaves. As they watched from the nearby hill, Black Tip agreed with Fang that it was going to be difficult for Hop-along and She-la to make their way through them. The goldfinches were still feeding on the thistle tops and if either got caught on a thistle, the birds would take flight. If that happened, it would surely give them away.

In fact the presence of the birds turned out to be a great help to Hop-along and She-la. As they made their way cautiously through the thistles they were aware of the birds above them, but if the birds were aware of them they weren't unduly concerned. They were too intent on plucking seeds from the thistle tops. In doing so they loosened many others that floated away in the breeze. And, as always happens when there is too much to choose from, they were continually moving from one patch to another. As a result, any disturbance caused to the birds went unnoticed. They quickly settled somewhere else, and any seed heads shaken loose by the passage of the foxes drifted away as nature intended.

On reaching the lower edge of the thistles, She-la watched as Hop-along hobbled down towards the geese. He only went a short distance at a time, availing of the cover of any weeds or clumps of grass he could find. The geese were stretching out their long necks to sift through the mud for any tiny morsel of food they could find and when they spotted him standing close by they moved away, squawking, but didn't go very far.

Up on the hill, the other red foxes and their three friends watched from the cover of the gorse as Hop-along lay down and rolled over on his back. His three legs and what remained of his fourth were sticking up in the air. It was a strange sight and one that made the captive foxes wonder what was going on.

'He's pretending to be dead,' Fang whispered.

'And why is he doing that?' asked Bluebell.

'He's using his cunning,' Black Tip told them. 'Something you all must do. Now just watch and learn.'

Down in The Field of Thistles, the geese continued to sift through the mud. The strange visitor to their field, it seemed, was not a threat to them. At the same time they were aware that he was there.

After a while, Hop-along rolled over on his side and let his tongue loll out as if he was dead. It was only a slight movement but some of the geese moved away. One goose, however, was curious. It went over to look. Hop-along didn't move. The goose ventured closer. It was almost within Hop-along's grasp, but he still didn't move. The goose stretched out its neck to have a closer look. Hop-along immediately caught it by the neck and started dragging it back up towards the thistles.

On the hill overlooking the field, the other foxes watched Hop-along's painful progress. It was obvious the dead goose was too heavy for him. Reaching a clump of rushes he slumped down. The geese that had been left behind were squawking loudly and flapping their wings. Fang made to rise but Black Tip stopped him, drawing his attention to two collie dogs that were roaming around the farmyard. 'We don't want to draw them onto him,' he whispered.

Fortunately the dogs were accustomed to hearing the

geese and paid them no heed. The farmer appeared at the gap in the hedge and looked around to see if anything was wrong. He didn't see Hop-along and the goose behind the clump of rushes. Nor did he notice that one of his geese was missing, and he went on about his business.

From her hiding place in the thistles, She-la was also watching Hop-along, anxious to help but waiting for the right moment to move. When the squawking of the geese brought no response from the farmyard, she broke cover and raced down towards the clump of rushes. Hop-along, she discovered, was still holding on to the goose, but unable to drag it any further. Grabbing it by the neck, she took over and started pulling it up the field. Able-bodied as she was, she also found it very heavy and had to leave it down to get her breath back. Hop-along, who by now had caught up with her, grabbed it by the neck and dragged it a few more paces. She-la took over again and in this relay fashion they managed to reach the safety of the thistles.

Leaving Black Tip to take the three farmed foxes back to the badger sett, Fang raced down the hill to help take the goose back. Which one had the more difficult job – Black Tip or Fang – was something they would laugh about later, for the goose had to be dragged and the other foxes coaxed every inch of the way. Nevertheless, they all got there and in the safety of the sett joined Old Sage Brush and Vickey in a feast that was big enough for all of them.

As the old fox gnawed on one of the few remaining bones, he licked his lips and told the farmed foxes, 'There is a saying in our world that if you're not strong you must be clever. We are not strong, but we have learned to be clever, and if we are weak like Hop-along, we must be very clever.' He licked his lips in a way that indicated he was happy in the knowledge that the three of them had just been given a valuable lesson, and taking up one of the bones retired to the inner recesses of the sett.

She-la, however, was far from happy. While her appetite was satisfied, she felt that Old Sage Brush had put her mate in danger unnecessarily. The foxes from the fur farm, she later told Vickey, could have been given the same lesson by showing them how to catch a rabbit. It was the kind of trick they often used in a remote field far from the eyes of man and from any danger.

Vickey nodded. She understood She-la's concern for Hop-along. At the same time she pointed out what Old Sage Brush had already done, that they needed something more substantial than a rabbit if they were all to eat.

Having retreated to a side tunnel to brood on what had happened, Hop-along also felt that while the reward had been good the risk had been too high. And for the first time he questioned the wisdom of Old Sage Brush. It was cunning they needed, not strength the old fox had said. However, cunning alone had not been enough in The Field of the

Thistles. To bring his trick to a successful conclusion he also needed strength. That was something he didn't have, and he realised that had it not been for She-la's prompt action, he himself might well have met the same fate as the goose.

SIX

THE SHEE FOX

There was little colour left in the countryside now. The wind had stripped most of the leaves from the trees and the cold had taken most of the flowers from the fields. Here and there a few stems of sturdy ragwort remained, not as tall or as yellow as in summer, but still as poisonous to the animals that grazed there. In greater abundance were dead spikes of rusty dock weed and it was these that provided cover for Old Sage Brush and his friends as they continued their journey to the Hills of the Long Low Cloud.

For cover in the hedgerows, the foxes sought out a plant that ancient man had once recorded as being king of the trees. Not a very imposing one, but the chosen one nevertheless. The olive, the fig and the vine, according to man's Holy Book, had refused the honour of being king, but the humble bramble had accepted, saying, '...if you anoint me king over you, then come and put your trust in my shadow.'

The foxes, of course, knew nothing of such lofty things, but it was in the shadow of the arching briars of the bramble that they now put their trust whenever they went to ground to escape the attentions of man.

From such a hiding place Old Sage Brush sent out the red foxes to secluded fields to show those of other colours how to be cunning and how to hunt. They taught them tricks to mesmerise and fool the rabbit; caution to avoid pursuit by the unrelenting stoat; and, perhaps most important of all, ways in which to stay out of the clutches of man. But it was Old Sage Brush who, as always, gave them words of wisdom.

It was on a river bank that the old fox had once taught cubs in the Land of Sinna an important lesson in the art of survival. They had been playful as all cubs are and had rushed into the water in an effort to catch small fish. When the fish scattered and they came out with nothing, he told them never to rush into the water; never to rush into anything, in fact, but to think, as there was always a better, safer way.

Snowflake, Bluebell and Nightshade were lying beside him looking at a heron which hadn't moved even when Black Tip pointed it out to them.

'Study the heron,' the old fox told them. 'Whenever it walks in the water, it steps lightly so as not to frighten the fish. And when it waits for the fish to come it doesn't move, no matter how long it takes. Even its eyes don't move. Yet it watches the water for fish and it watches the bank for danger.'

The old fox stroked his grey whiskers with his paw, adding, 'As you go out to hunt, you will do well to do as the heron does. Step lightly, look to the front and glance to each side. That may seem a simple thing to do. But it is the simple things that can make the difference between life and death.'

Hop-along, who was lying nearby, watched and listened. There was much to be said for the advice the old fox was giving them. However, his encounter with the geese in The Field of Thistles had made him sceptical and he said to himself that it would take more than words of wisdom to turn the foxes of many colours into red foxes.

★ ★ ★

The trapper kneeled and looked at the paw prints. Then getting to his feet he smiled and rubbed the paw that hung around his neck. His father, who had taught him how to hunt, had worn a rabbit's paw around his neck for luck. Now, as the trapper of foxes, he wore a fox's paw. Not that he was superstitious. He left that to those of an older generation.

He didn't believe, as some of the older people did, that they must carry a stick when walking through the fields in case a badger caught them by the leg. They believed that the badger wouldn't let go until it heard the crack of the stick being broken, thinking it was the crack of the bone. He knew the jaws of the badger were exceedingly strong, but he had never heard of a badger catching anyone by the leg.

He didn't believe that stoats hunted in packs and would attack people, for he had never seen it. Nor did he believe that bats were vampires, or that if one got caught in a person's hair the only way to get it out was to cut the hair off. Not that he himself had much hair.

He didn't believe in fairies, or the shee as they were called in Gaelic, or that the banshee was a wizened old fairy woman whose cries at night foretold a death. He knew that the cries were those of a vixen, but the older people refused to believe him.

He didn't believe that the will-o'-the-wisp that lured people off their paths and into bogs was either a ghost or a fairy fire. In his view it was some kind of gas that flickered on the bogs at night. Not something supernatural, but something to be avoided all the same.

He didn't salute a magpie to ward off the superstition that one for was for sorrow, or look for a second in the belief that it was for joy. However, he did believe that when he heard the excited chattering of magpies and saw them mobbing something in a nearby field, the object of their attention was more than likely a fox.

The trapper pushed back his greasy cap and lit a cigarette.

The paw prints and the magpies were all he needed to catch up with the foxes that had fled from Glensinna, and with luck he would do so soon.

★ ★ ★

It wouldn't be long before the magpies did bring danger upon the foxes as they traversed the fields, but it wouldn't come from the trapper – at least, not yet.

On Vickey's advice, they had decided to rest up for a while in the earth beneath the briars. She could see that Old Sage Brush and Hop-along tired easily, while hunting for food and showing the farmed foxes how to do so was taking a lot out of the others.

When the shooters combed the fields for pheasants and the meadows for duck they left little behind. Some of the birds returned with the fall of darkness, but were frightened and edgy and Black Tip and Fang found them difficult to catch. Fortunately, the shooters were only interested in game and didn't cover the same fields twice. When they moved on and the shooting became a distant sound, rabbits which had had retreated to the safety of their burrows came out – and so did the foxes.

It was then that the farmed foxes learned there was more to hunting than they thought. Rabbits were always on the look-out for danger and not as easy to catch as they imagined. Hares were too fast and sleeping hedgehogs too prickly. Small birds always took flight, while magpies would seek out the fox and were almost impossible to catch.

Even Old Sage Brush with all his wisdom could not advise them on how to deal with magpies that mobbed them, apart from the fact that they should retreat to the nearest hedge and wait for them to go away. However, he did make the point that magpies mobbed other creatures too and on occasion could lead them to food.

When they were fed up with rabbit they all agreed that they should move on. It was coming on towards dusk and Old Sage Brush decided that they should travel by what daylight remained so that they could teach the farmed foxes as they went along. As always, he used Black Tip as his eyes and asked him to scout ahead for any sign of danger, while getting Fang to hang back and made sure they weren't being followed.

Everything went well until Black Tip heard a commotion on the other side of a hedge. Peering through it, he saw he was at the side of a road. Magpies and rooks were flitting up and down, pecking at something furry, but he couldn't make out what it was. When he reported back to the others they immediately took cover, then retreated a short distance to consider the situation.

'What do you think?' asked Old Sage Brush. 'Are they mobbing one of ours?'

'It's difficult to say,' Black Tip replied. 'They could have spotted a fox trying to cross.'

'Or one that's been injured by man's machines,' said Fang, who had come up to join them.

'Any sign of man?' asked the old fox.

'Not that I could see,' replied Black Tip.

'Then what are we afraid of?' said the old fox. 'Let's find out what the magpies are at.'

'Do you think that's wise?' asked She-la. 'We don't want to bring trouble upon ourselves.'

'If one of our kind is in trouble,' said Vickey, 'then we must draw them off.'

The old fox nodded. 'That's what I was going to ask Fang to do. If we can get to the cover of the hedge without the magpies seeing us, and wait there until he has drawn them off, then we have a better chance of crossing without being seen – and maybe help the other fox when they're not looking.'

'We must be careful we don't end up the same way,' Hop-long cautioned. 'Many of our kind have been hit by man's machines – badgers too – and few of them have lived to tell the tale.'

Old Sage Brush nodded. 'That's true. But they were solitary foxes. They had no one else to look out for them. We do.'

Using every hedge and ditch as cover, Black Tip led them to the field at the side of the road. Seeing gulls circling the area, he said, 'The gok-goks have arrived, so there's some-thing in trouble all right.'

The magpies and rooks were still mobbing whatever they had found and Fang crept along the hedge until he was as close them as he dared.

'Well?' asked the old fox when he returned.

'It's not a fox,' Fang told him. 'It's a hare. But they're not mobbing it. It's dead.'

'Ah. Food!'

At that precise moment the old fox's carefully laid plans descended into chaos. As he said the word 'food' they heard the sound of one of man's machines bearing down on them. The three farmed foxes immediately broke away from the rest of them and rushed through the hedge on to the road. There was a deafening squeal of tyres as the driver swerved to avoid them. Fang rushed after them and knocked Snow-flake over, yelling, 'What do you think you're doing? Get back into cover before you get killed.'

Picking herself up, Snowflake watched man's machine speed away and its tail lights fade in the distance.

'Come on,' Fang shouted again. 'Get back into cover.'

While all this was going on, Black Tip was hurredly lead-ing the others back the way they had come. Fang and the farm foxes followed, and they didn't stop until they were safely in the earth in the shadow of the briars.

The magpies had taken flight, only to land on a nearby

hedge. With their long tails flicking, they watched the foxes going back the way they had come. Normally they would have followed the foxes and tormented them until they took cover. However, the rooks had already returned to the road and were pecking at the dead hare. A dead hare, they decided, was more important than a live fox, and they weren't about to leave it to the rooks.

Old Sage Brush and his group were badly shaken by what had happened.

'What did you think you were doing?' Black Tip demanded.

Snowflake was crestfallen. 'It was when we heard the word food.'

'And heard man's machine coming,' said Bluebell. 'We thought he was coming to feed us.'

'You're not in a cage now!' Fang declared. 'Those machines don't feed, they kill.'

'You might have got us all killed,' Hop-along added.

Bluebell lowered her head saying, 'Sorry.'

There was silence for a moment as they all contemplated what had happened and what might have happened.

'Flithengibbers,' said Black Tip, cursing the magpies beneath his breath.

'Were we followed?' asked Old Sage Brush.

'No,' Fang told him. 'It's dark now.'

'Good.' There was silence again until the old fox added, 'The magpies will be gone. Why don't you go back and get what remains of the hare? It'll be a change from rabbit.'

★ ★ ★

In the nights that followed, the three farmed foxes watched as the Great Running Fox in the Sky came down to touch the new world in which they had found themselves. As they talked, Vickey told them how to mark the spot before it took off again on its own nightly journey. If they did that, she assured them, they would not lose their way. It was one of many secrets known only to the red foxes, and the farmed foxes learned many more as their friends tried to help them adapt to life in the wild.

Whatever about the others, Hop-along was again beginning to question the wisdom of Old Sage Brush. They had followed him on long journeys before and while they had been quick to learn from him, the three farmed foxes were slow to learn. Their ancestors might have passed some things down to them, but not the basic instincts of the wild fox, especially cunning on which that instinct of survival was based. It was like herding sheep that had no idea where to go or how to get there, and that was putting them all in danger.

Then, Hop-along thought, maybe it wasn't the three farmed foxes that were putting them in danger. Maybe it was the old fox, insisting that they make an impossible journey and perform impossible tasks along the way. If only he could see the way these three foxes behaved, but he couldn't. To him a fox was a fox and in his mind's eye he could see no reason why they shouldn't be taught to act like a fox.

When they were lying up during the day, Hop-along shared his concerns with his mate. She-la might have thought he was moaning about things because of his handicap, but she had to agree with him. The journey was becoming very difficult and Old Sage Brush wasn't making it any easier for any of them. She in turned shared her thoughts with the others and it wasn't long before doubts about what the old fox was doing began creeping into the minds of Fang and Black Tip.

Even Vickey on whom the old fox depended for inspiration in times of hardship, began to wonder if they were doing the right thing. Sage Brush was much older now than he had been on their previous journeys and she wondered if, perhaps, there was some merit in their murmurings. Could it be that the old fox was past the stage where his guidance was sound and his words of wisdom something to be valued? Were they just the ramblings of an old fox?

Having discussed the matter with Black Tip, Vickey decided that she must tell Old Sage Brush about the questions that had now arisen in their minds about what they were doing and where they were going. Fang, Black Tip and She-la were, as usual, doing the hunting, and the rest of them were lying in undergrowth in a wood listening to the sounds of the night

When Vickey had finished, Old Sage Brush slowly stroked his grey whiskers as he always did when he was deep in thought. She had told him in a way she hoped would cause him least offence and as she waited for him to respond, she wondered what he would say. As always, it wasn't what she expected.

'It is only when we are half way through a wood that we can expect to see what lies on the other side,' he told her. 'Perhaps it is time to show them what they cannot see.'

Vickey realised that the old fox, in his own quaint way, wasn't talking about the wood they were now in, but their lack of faith.

One by one, Fang, Black Tip and She-la returned to say they had failed to find anything on their hunting trips. Here and there in the wood they had come across houses with hens, but they had found no way into the coops and were afraid of drawing the wrath of man and his dogs upon them.

Old Sage Brush nodded. Normally, he knew, they would have risked finding a way into the hens, but it was the safety of himself and Hop-along and the farmed foxes that had prevented them doing so.

'You did right,' he told them, 'but there is a way. Return to one of the houses but do not approach the hens. Stay back in the woods and, She-la, you let man hear the call of the vixen.'

'And then what?' asked Black Tip.

'Just wait,' said the old fox, 'and see what happens.'

'That could be dangerous,' said Fang.

'Not if you stay back far enough to be out of range of his guns but close enough to see what happens.'

Reluctantly, Black Tip, Fang and She-la did what the old fox said. They were apprehensive, but curious to find out what he had in mind. When they were in what they judged to be a safe position some distance from a house, She-la uttered the piercing scream of a vixen at mating time. Nothing happened. She did it again. And again. This time lights came on and a dark figure ran from the house to where the hens were cackling uneasily at the sound of the fox. At the edge of darkness he raised his gun and fired blindly into the woods.

'So much for that,' said Fang. 'Let's get out of here.'

Old Sage Brush, however, showed no surprise and told them to approach another house and do the same.

Once again lights came on and dogs bounded out to the rim of light, barking loudly. Fortunately, the dogs came no farther than the edge of darkness, and the three foxes returned to their den.

'Sage Brush,' said Black Tip, 'this is madness.'

'We're letting man know we are in the woods,' said Fang, 'and we're not getting near his hens.'

'We also risk drawing his dogs upon us,' added She-la.

'I would ask you to go to another house and do the same,' replied Old Sage Brush, 'but I fear that you fear for us more than you fear for yourselves. That being the case, I will go. Now who will show me the way?'

Black Tip stepped closer to him saying, 'You know I have always been your eyes.'

'If you're going, so am I,' said Vickey.

'And what about one of our friends? Nightshade, you will not be easily seen, perhaps you will come too.'

Nightshade scurried forward, eager to go and unaware of the danger in doing so.

The other red foxes were sure now that Old Sage Brush had take leave of his senses, but their protests went unheeded.

'If some of you wish to follow, do,' the old fox told them, 'but at a safe distance.'

Black Tip led the way to yet a third house. It was a cottage at the edge of the woods and like the other houses, had a number of hens in a netting wire coop in the back garden.

'Now Nightshade,' said the old fox, 'let them hear the call of the vixen.'

Nightshade raised her head and opened her mouth, but nothing came. She coughed to cover her embarrassment, saying, 'I'm sorry, but I have never called a mate.'

With some trepidation Vickey raised her head and screamed. Nothing happened down at the house and she told Nightshade, 'Now you try it.'

Nightshade managed to scream, though not very loudly, and Vickey screamed again.

This time a light came on in the yard of the house and an elderly man looked out but he didn't go any farther. Instead he turned off the light and went inside.

Vickey gave one more blood-curdling scream and when there was no further response at the house Old Sage Brush told them the way was clear.

Black Tip fetched Fang and She-la and together they burrowed their way in under the netting wire of the coop. The hens were cackling and flapping around inside, but still no one came from the house to see what was wrong.

'Only take what you need,' Old Sage Brush had warned, and that's what they did.

★ ★ ★

'You're lucky,' the trapper said the next day when he called to see the elderly couple who lived in the cottage. 'They could have cleaned you out.'

'It was the cry of the banshee,' the old woman told him. 'We heard it several times.'

'There's no such thing,' the trapper told her. 'All you heard was the cry of a vixen.'

'It was a banshee,' the old man assured him. 'And mark my words, it foretells a death.'

The trapper smiled. He had spoken to several people in the area in his efforts to track down the foxes. Some had chased them away with their guns and dogs, but superstition had kept this elderly couple indoors. They would still believe that death would follow the cry of the banshee, but he knew only too well that the only death the vixen had foretold was the death of the couple's hens.

SEVEN

CATCHING
SNOWFLAKES

Whe hen daylight came, some of the people who had
heard the calls of the vixens took out their guns and dogs and
set out in search of the predators. They knew that other foxes,
especially dog foxes, would answer the calls, and already the
chicken coop of one house had been raided. However, the
foxes who had struck in the middle of the night were long
gone.

Old Sage Brush and his fellow foxes had left the wood
behind and were now in hilly country some distance beyond
it. On the sides of the hills grew shrubs which earlier in
the year had borne small edible fruits known in Ireland as
fraughans and elsewhere as bilberries or blueberries.

The shrubs gave the foxes some cover, but not enough. Furthermore, the sky had clouded over during the night and a light scattering of snow had given the grass and shrubs a tinge of white. If it continued to snow, their tracks would be clearly visible.

'We must find cover below ground,' said Old Sage Brush.

'I think I've hunted around here before,' Fang told him. 'Perhaps I can find an earth that's not occupied.'

'Good,' said the old fox. 'There must be foxes who live in this area. Maybe they can help us.'

As the others huddled together for warmth, the three farmed foxes relaxed in the mistaken belief that there was safety in numbers. However, the old fox knew otherwise and told Fang to hurry.

It wasn't another fox but a badger that Fang came across. It was a young female and instead of being aggressive as he had come to expect of badgers, this one appeared to be frightened.

The young badger, it transpired, had strayed too far from her sett. She couldn't find her way back and now that daylight had come, found herself out in the open, alone and vulnerable. It was obvious she needed help, but Fang was uncertain what he should do. He and his friends had an uneasy relationship with her kind. He had once been hurled out of a sett by a boar badger and ever since had given them a wide berth. They were, he realised, intensely private animals and resented any intrusion of their space. On the other hand, there had been occasions when fox and badger had found it expedient to help one another.

This seemed to Fang to be such an occasion, so he told the young badger to follow him and he would try and help her find her sett. His sense of smell, he reckoned, was better than hers. In addition, he could see what her small eyes, perhaps, could not see. She had left many circles of paw prints on the powdery snow that now covered the grass. If he could disentangle them, he might be able to determine where she had come from.

It was a difficult task and one that was not without its dangers. Light and all as the snowfall had been, Fang realised that the more he disturbed the snow the less obvious the badger's tracks became to him, but the more obvious his tracks became to man. Nevertheless, he persevered and eventually found himself looking up at a tree-covered hillock, or mound, which was peppered with holes that been excavated by badgers.

'This is it!' the young badger exclaimed and, racing up the hill, disappeared into one of the holes.

Fang was about to go when the young badger reappeared and called him back. She was followed by another older badger, who said, 'She tells me you guided her back to the sett. Thank you.'

Fang shrugged. 'It was the least I could do.'

As the young badger galloped back into the sett, the other said, 'She was the last of my litter and very weak. Somehow she didn't develop as fast the others, and even now when the time is coming when she should be thinking of having cubs of her own, she is still very dependent on me. I thought she was having a long sleep with the rest of us, but when I awoke she was gone.'

'Do you have a long sleep like the hedgehog?' asked Fang.

The mother badger smiled. 'No, but sometimes when ice grips the streams and frost hardens the fields, it can be very difficult to forage for food. So we go down into our sett where the cold cannot reach us and go into a deep sleep – but only until we feel like eating again.'

Fang was aware that when the weather got very cold, hedgehogs curled up and slept until it got warmer again. However, it was news to him that badgers might also go into a deep sleep, if only for a few days.

'When the nights were warm and the rest of my cubs wanted to go out to the fields to play,' the mother badger went on, 'she wanted to stay in the sett and sleep. And now when it's cold and we want to sleep, she decides to go out in the snow and gets lost.'

Fang turned to go, saying, 'She'll learn.'

The mother badger smiled. 'She's almost fully grown, but she's still my cub, and you were good enough to bring her back. The least I can do is ask you to come in.'

It was a rare invitation and one that Fang wasn't about to turn down. He and his friends were in a predicament and he had not come across any other foxes that might help. The mound, he found, had been the home of generations of badgers and contained numerous tunnels and chambers. However, many of the chambers were empty.

'Man continues to kill many of our kind,' the mother badger told him. 'Why he does so, I do not know. We don't bother him by day and during the night we seek nothing from his fields but worms and beetles.'

'He hunts us too,' Fang replied. 'We take his hens because we need food and he takes our coats to keep himself warm.'

Fang then told her the story of the foxes that were being farmed for their fur, and how he and his friends were trying to find them a new home.

'I have heard it said that foxes once helped some of our kind to find a new home,' said the mother badger. 'If your friends have found themselves out in the open as my young one did, then they are welcome to come and stay here.'

Fang nodded. He was one of the foxes who had helped the badgers. But it was a story that would have to wait. Old Sage Brush and the others were still out in the open, waiting for him to bring them to safety.

'I thank you for your offer,' he told the mother badger, 'but if man has been killing badgers from this sett, how can it be safe for us?'

'The danger has passed,' she assured him. 'Man will leave the rest of us alone – until the next time.'

'And when might that be?'

'Those of us who have survived have come to know when to expect him and have worked out ways to avoid him. So, rest assured, you will be safe.'

Fang nodded, but like the mother badger he was puzzled by man's actions in killing the badgers. He couldn't know, of course, that some members of mankind were equally puzzled. The periodic culling of badgers was carried out in certain areas in the belief that as they sniffed around the fields at night they spread a disease called TB to cattle. Many believed that the disease was spread by the cattle themselves and that the badger was not to blame, but the killing continued.

Taking the mother badger's word for it that the danger had now passed and that the sett would provide his friends with a place of refuge, Fang thanked her and left. Outside he paused and looked up. The sky was heavy with cloud and he sensed it was laden with snow. He must hurry. If he got the others back to the sett before it began to snow again, then the snow would cover their tracks and they would be safe.

★ ★ ★

'Why did you call us flithengibbers?' asked Snowflake.

They were all curled up together in the Mound of the Badgers.

'It wasn't the three of you I called flithengibbers,' Black Tip whispered. 'It was the magpies.'

'Oh. And why did you call them that?'

'It's not a word we're supposed to use. It's a bad word, but I was annoyed.' Black Tip paused. 'I was cursing them for putting us in danger.'

'But it was us who put you in danger, not the magpies,' said Nightshade.

'If the magpies hadn't been there in the first place, we wouldn't have had to go sneaking around the way we did.'

'And tell me,' said Snowflake, 'are magpies black with white patches or white with black patches?'

'I don't know,' Black Tip admitted. 'What do you think Fang?'

'A bit of both, I suppose.'

Hop-along, who was lying nearby said, 'If you find the feather of a magpie you will see many colours in it.'

'And the badgers,' persisted Snowflake. 'Is their head black with white stripes or white with black stripes?'

'I've no idea,' said Black Tip. 'I suppose I never really thought about it.'

Vickey, who had overheard the conversation, disappeared into the nearest tunnel and when she returned, she informed them, 'The mother badger says they are white with black stripes.'

'There you are,' said Black Tip. 'You have it from the

badger's own mouth.'

'But their paws are black,' Snowflake continued.

'So are ours,' said Fang.

'Yours are black,' Snowflake said. 'Mine are white.'

'It doesn't matter if the paws are black or white, so long as they can catch a mouse,' said a voice from nearby. Old Sage Brush, who had been dozing in another tunnel, had just joined them. As he lay down beside them, he asked, 'What's it like outside?'

'It's beginning to snow again,' Fang told him.

'Then now might be a good time to hunt.'

'I'll go,' said Black Tip.

Vickey got up. 'Me too.'

'Me too,' said She-la.

The old fox shook his head. 'Leave it to Black Tip and Fang. Too many of you would leave too many tracks in the snow. Anyway, She-la, you and Vickey did your share back in the wood. Man, I imagine, has never heard the call of a vixen to equal yours. Yours too Nightshade. It was truly worthy of a wild fox.'

'But what happened?' Hop-along asked. 'We still don't understand it.'

'It was something that perhaps only a fox of my years has learned and yet, even I do not understand it.' The old fox paused. 'Before man robbed me of my sight, I searched around many of his chicken coops to see if I could find a way in. More often than not I was driven away, but I noticed that occasionally, especially during our mating time, when man heard the cry of a vixen he went inside and didn't come out again. It was almost as if the cry of the vixen had frightened him.'

'How very strange,' said Black Tip.

Fang shook his head. 'I have never heard of such a thing, and I wouldn't have believed it if I hadn't seen it with my own eyes.'

'And don't you see,' said She-la. 'Ratwiddle's prediction has come true, or at least part of it. What was it he said now? Yes, he said man would fear the fox.'

Hop-along grunted. 'He also said the fox would hunt the man. Somehow I can't see that happening.'

'Many things that seem impossible are possible,' the old fox told them. 'I suppose they just require a little more patience.'

Hop-along and the others knew that Old Sage Brush was giving them a gentle rebuke for their lack of faith in him.

'We… I… thought,' Hop-along began.

'We were beginning to think… Well… a…' Black Tip couldn't put into words either the guilt he now felt. Nor could Fang.

Vickey intervened. 'What they're trying to say is that they're sorry for doubting you. Isn't that right?'

The mumbled apology that followed wasn't very clear, but Old Sage Brush didn't quibble with it. 'It's not what is left behind, but what is left that is important,' was all he said.

That may have sounded ungrateful, but the more the others thought about it, they realised that as usual the old fox's words were few but full of meaning. And if they were waiting for him to elaborate, he didn't. Instead, he got up and left them to work it out for themselves.

'I think,' said Vickey when he had gone, 'he means that while some of us might have lost faith in him before, we probably have more faith in him now than ever.'

'We shouldn't have doubted him in the first place,' said Hop-along. 'I suppose it was my fault.'

'You had more reason to doubt him than we had,' She-la assured him.

'And I'm sure he has more faith in you now, than any of us,' added Vickey. 'That was a very brave thing you did in the Field of the Thistles.'

'He didn't mind putting himself in danger,' Hop-along recalled, 'and he is less able than any of us.'

'Well, it's all over now,' Vickey told him. 'As soon as the snow clears we'll keep going. The Hills of the Long Low Cloud can't be too far away.'

Black Tip went out to hunt first, followed a short time later by Fang. However, they found very little. Timid as always, the rabbits were reluctant to venture far from their burrows to find out why their grass was white instead of green. The pheasants were content to sit tight while the snow added another layer of cover to their hiding places. The small birds of the hedgerows looked down for a place to search for food and, seeing none, decided to stay where they were.

★ ★ ★

Another searcher, however, was looking down at the snow and he found what he was looking for – fox prints. Before they were covered by the falling snow, the trapper could see that they came and went from the badger sett. As long as the foxes stayed there he couldn't catch them. Too many entrances, too many exits. But foxes, he knew, were creatures of habit. They were inclined to follow the same paths and he felt sure that those in the badger sett would do the same.

★ ★ ★

Inside the sett, all the foxes bar two were curled up, sharing their warmth and dreaming of food. Fang had gone out hunting again and Snowflake was lying at the entrance looking out at this thing they called snow that made the semi-darkness of the dawn so bright. Only a few flakes were falling now – these things from which, she had been told, she got her name – and she was curious to see what they were like when they landed. But when she reached out and caught them on her paw, they melted, and when they fell on the snow they ceased to be snowflakes.

Oblivious to any danger that might be out there, Snowflake charged down the heap of earth that had been excavated by the badgers and tumbled out onto the carpet of snow. She wondered what it tasted like, but found it melted in her mouth and turned to water. She sank into it, yet discovered that it gave way to a peculiar crunchiness as she rolled and frolicked like a kitten that had just found the fun that was to be had with a ball of wool.

Snowflake also found that wherever she went and whatever she did, whether rolling or jumping or running, she left an imprint on the snow. It was so soft, so different from the hard wire she had walked on in her previous life, and she loved it. Then she spotted the paw prints of the foxes that had been out hunting. Some of them were almost obscured by the falling snow, but one set was fresh and she galloped after them, wondering in her excitement whose they were and where they led to.

Snowflake had forgotten that Fang had gone out hunting again, but more importantly she had forgotten the little she had learned, especially the advice she had been given by Old Sage Brush. 'Step lightly,' he had cautioned her. 'Look to the front and glance to each side.' She did none of these things. Instead she bounded down the field looking only at the paw prints in the snow. And when she followed them through a hole in the hedge, she became entangled in a net from which she found there was no escape. It was a fine net but very strong and had been strung across the hole like a spider's web.

Fang had hunted far and near without success. The snow had given the landscape a very different appearance, but he recognised some of the features. Not far from the Mound of the Badgers were fields where he had once watched geese flying in to feed. He had caught one or two and dined well. But not now. Nothing moved in this unreal world of white, or so it seemed. Then he spotted magpies a short distance ahead of him. They were flitting around something, chattering and squawking as they always did when they found food or some creature in distress. This time it wasn't food. The creature in distress, he could see, was white. He stopped in his tracks. It was Snowflake.

In her efforts to get free, Snowflake had dispersed the snow from the ditch and could be clearly seen against the green of the grass and the brown of the soil. Her wriggling and writhing were not something to be missed by the magpies, and the net gave her no protection from them.

Fang was about to go to her assistance when a familiar smell assailed his nostrils. It wasn't the smell of pheasant or rabbit, but one he detested. It gave him an acrid twinge in his nostrils and a feeling of fear, for he knew from experience that the smell came from man. Not any man, but the trapper. He immediately retreated to the cover of a hedge where he could observe what was going on without being seen.

Not far from where the commotion was taking place, Fang could now see the trapper. The tell-tale smoke that had warned him of the man's presence was coming from his mouth. Shooing the magpies away with a wave of his hand the trapper reached into his bag and took out a sack. Snowflake was now so enmeshed in the net that she had ceased to struggle. The trapper released the net where it was fastened to the hedge, pulled it tight and dropped Snowflake, net and all into the sack. Powerless to do anything, Fang watched in dismay as the trapper slung the sack over his shoulder and strode off across the snow-covered fields.

EIGHT

THE TROPHY

Fang was frantic. His impulse was to follow the trapper. Then he thought he should tell the others first. Racing back to the badger sett, he blurted out the bad news. Startled, some of them retreated to the adjoining tunnels where they had been sleeping.

Realising they were afraid the trapper might come back for them', Old Sage Brush sought to reassure them. 'From what you say, Fang, I take it he didn't have any dogs with him.'

'No, he was on his own.'

'Then he can't touch us in here. And I doubt if he can put nets on all the entrances and exits – there are too many of them.'

'But what's going to happen to Snowflake?' asked Night-shade.

'Be thankful she was caught in a net, not a choking hedge-trap,' said the old fox.

'Or the snapping jaws,' added Hop-along.

'Maybe he's going to take her back to the cages,' cried Bluebell.

When no one sought to reassure her about that, Fang said, 'The trapper must have seen our tracks in the snow.'

'Well, if he can follow us,' said the old fox, 'we can follow him.'

'I'll go,' offered Black Tip.

'No,' said Fang. 'It was probably my tracks that led her into the trap.'

'Why don't you both go,' suggested the old fox. 'You'd better hurry before the falling snow covers his tracks – and be careful he doesn't lead you into another trap.'

In normal circumstances Black Tip and Fang would have left by the main entrance, but not now. They knew from experience that the trapper was smart. He was capable of doubling back and watching for them, even putting up more nets in the expectation that they might make the same mistake as Snowflake. So they went up to one of the smaller rear exits the badgers used to take their bedding out to dry, and crept out. They saw no footprints in the snow around the mound, so they went down to the hedge where Snowflake had been caught.

The trapper, they could see, had not turned back but had

trudged straight across the fields, and they had a great urge to race after him and try and catch sight of him. Instead they followed his footprints cautiously, looking out for any sign that he might have laid down a snapping jaws in the snow or a choking trap in the hedgerows.

The trapper, however, was on a mission. He wanted to catch the foxes that had escaped from the fur farm, alive and uninjured, so that he might sell them to another farm. The red foxes he would deal with in the usual way when he considered the time was right.

Black Tip and Fang found that the trapper's tracks led to a farmstead. From the cover of a nearby hedge they saw several people gathered around a small flat-bed truck that was parked in the yard. Two collie dogs were running around the truck, barking furiously and the watching foxes guessed that the trapper was showing off his trophy.

'What are we going to do?' wondered Black Tip.

'There's nothing we can do,' Fang replied, 'except watch and see what happens.'

'What if the dogs get our scent?'

'They're too close to Snowflake to get any scent but hers.'

As the people moved around the back of the truck to a get a better look at the white fox, Black Tip and Fang saw that the trapper had put Snowflake in a wire cage. Having escaped from such a cage only recently, they could just imagine the fear she must be feeling. Yet there was nothing they could do but sit tight and watch.

After a while they saw the trapper putting something on his hands. Then he opened the cage and took the cringing Snowflake out. She began snapping at him, but her sharp teeth were unable to penetrate his gloves and somehow he managed to put a collar on her neck. There was a leash attached to the collar and, holding her up by the leash and the tail, he walked around so that his friends could have a good look at her.

If that wasn't enough, the trapper took a long stick from the back of the truck and, placing the forked end of it behind the collar, put Snowflake down. Pinned almost to the concrete yard by the forked stick, she was forced to let him lead her around like a dog. The dogs themselves were now in such a high state of excitement that one of the men hauled them away and put them in a shed.

Black Tip and Fang watched, heartbroken by what was being done to such a lovely, gentle creature. Eventually the trapper put her back in the cage and carried it over to a barn a short distance away. There the other men watched as he secured the catch on the door of the cage with a piece of wire, before lifting it up on to a pile of bales. A few minutes later they all withdrew. One of them pulled the big sliding door closed and they all went into the house, laughing as they did so.

'Stay here,' Fang whispered.

Before Black Tip could say anything, Fang ran off and circled around until he came to the far side of the barn. The sides of the barn were made from old sheets of corrugated iron. Where water had been dripping down from a broken gutter, one of the sheets had rusted away at the bottom. Squeezing in through the jagged hole, Fang jumped up on to the bales and hopped across to where the trapper had left the cage.

'Snowflake,' he whispered. 'It's me, Fang. Are you all right?'

It was obvious that Snowflake wasn't all right. She was curled up in a corner of the cage, shivering and very frightened.

'Don't worry,' he assured her, 'I've loosened a trapper's wire before.'

As Fang clamped his teeth on the wire securing the clasp on the door and began to struggle with it, Snowflake shuffled over to him, saying, 'You're very brave, but I don't want you to get caught too.'

Fang stopped. 'Black Tip's keeping watch. He'll let us know if there's any danger.'

'The wire looks very strong. I don't see how you can break it.'

The wire, Fang discovered, was indeed very strong. It wasn't like the more flexible wire a trapper had once used to snare his friend, Black Tip. It was thicker and the two ends of it had been twisted around one another. No matter how much he tried he couldn't undo it or break it.

Not wishing to alarm Snowflake by admitting defeat, Fang just said, 'I'll be back in a minute,' and disappeared through the hole in the barn wall.

When he returned to where Black Tip was lying patiently waiting for him, he panted, 'The door of the cage. It's tied with very strong wire. I can't get it off, but maybe if we took turns at it we might be able to do it.'

As they hurried around to Snowflake, Black Tip thought of the time he had caught his neck in a choking hedge-trap. The wire had become deeply embedded in his neck because of all the struggling he had done and all attempts by his friends to remove it had failed. Then Fang had tried and he had lived up to his name. Somehow he had managed to get one of his long fangs in under the wire and that was all that was needed. The wire had loosened and he had been set free. But if Fang couldn't do it this time he feared there was little hope for Snowflake.

When they reached the hole in the barn wall, Black Tip said, 'Maybe you loosened the wire a little bit. I'll see if I can loosen it a bit more.'

Fang nodded. 'Ok. I'll keep a look out for the dogs. If they're let out I'll try and draw them off.'

Black Tip hopped up on to the bales and was about to approach the cage when someone began pulling back the big sliding door. Stepping lightly, he climbed up into the dark recesses of the barn and from there watched as the trapper came in and checked that the white fox was still securely caged. He saw nothing to indicate that another fox had been gnawing at the wire holding the catch in place and left.

As soon as the great sliding was closed, Black Tip went down to the cage. If Snowflake saw him, she gave no flicker of recognition and he guessed the return of the trapper had renewed all her fears. He immediately attacked the wire and even managed to get one of his front teeth down between the strands. More than that, however, he could not do.

Fang came in and took over, but try as they would and taking turns to give one another a rest, they couldn't get the wire to budge.

Realising at last that they were wasting their time, Fang told Snowflake that they would be have to go, but promised they would be back.

'Please don't leave me,' she pleaded.

'It's only for a little while,' he assured her. 'There must be a way to open the cage, but we must think about it.'

'Please hurry,' she cried. 'Please, before the trapper comes back.'

Fang promised once more that he wouldn't desert her and went outside. 'It's no use,' he told Black Tip. 'We're going to have to think of something else.'

They returned to the hedge where they could continue to keep the farmyard under observation.

'Do you think the vixens could help us?' asked Fang. 'We could take it in turns again.'

Black Tip ran his tongue around his top teeth. 'Look. You're the one with the really strong teeth. If you can't do it, none of us can. And I don't know about you, but my teeth are sore. So are my jaws.'

Fang nodded. 'Mine too.'

'You'd need to have the jaws of a badger to open that wire,' Black Tip added ruefully.

'A badger,' exclaimed Fang. 'That's it! Maybe the badgers can help us.'

Black Tip nodded. 'We could ask the mother badger, I suppose. She might be willing to help. After all, you helped her cub.'

'And in return for that she allowed us to stay in the sett.'

'Still, she might help us again. It's our only hope.' Black Tip paused. 'If you keep an eye on Snowflake, I'll go and ask her.'

Shortly after Black Tip left, the men emerged from the house. The farmer let the two collies out of the shed, tapped the ground with a long walking stick to bring them to heel, and went up the fields with them.

Fang breathed a sigh of relief. He had seen dogs like that herding sheep, and knew they were accustomed to doing what they were told.

When the other men left, the trapper climbed up on to

the back of the truck and began separating an assortment of nets, snares and metal traps, a number of which he put into his bag. He also took a dead chicken from under a cover and dropped it into the bag. Then he went over to the barn and slid open the door. Anxiously Fang watched to see what he was going to do. If he took Snowflake away on the truck, that would be the end of it. Fortunately he emerged without her and closed the door. Returning to the truck he took out the bag of traps, slung it over his shoulder and left the yard.

Fang crept along the bottom of the hedge to see where the trapper was going. If he retraced his steps he would walk straight into Black Tip and the badger.

Fang, it might be said, wasn't a great believer in foxlore. He didn't really believe in the Great White Fox but, like many other foxes, he did so in times of trouble. And not for the first time that morning he now had cause to thank the Great White Fox for its protection. For instead of heading for the badger sett, the trapper set off in a different direction. It seemed he had something else in mind and his day's work was far from over.

The wintry sun was up now and the steady drops of water from the branches above told Fang that a thaw was on the way. With luck, he thought, it would come soon as snow made their tracks too easy to follow. He ran around to the back of the barn and told Snowflake that help was on the way.

'Thank you,' she whispered. 'I was beginning to think you weren't coming back.'

Fang smiled. 'I told you I'd be back, and I'll stay with you now until the badger comes.'

Fang did his best to comfort Snowflake, while hoping against hope that the badger would indeed come. And come she did.

A short time later Black Tip came in through the hole in the side of the barn and Fang was relieved to see the badger squeezing in after him.

'You're very good to come,' he told her.

'You saved the life of my cub,' she panted. 'The least I can do is to try and save the life of your friend.'

'Are the dogs still in the shed?' asked Black Tip.

Fang shook his head. 'No, they've gone up the fields with the farmer.'

'And the trapper?'

'He's gone too.'

'Where?' asked the badger.

'It's okay. He hasn't gone back to your sett – he went in a different direction.'

'It's just as well,' said Black Tip, 'or we'd have run straight into him.'

'Well, we're here now,' the badger said. 'Show me what you want me to do.'

The mother badger looked closely at the twisted wire.

Her small eyes were more accustomed to the nightly ritual of turning over cow pats and looking for beetles. Nevertheless she could see the way the trapper had twisted the ends of the wire around one another. Clamping her teeth on them, she turned her body over and over in the same way that a crocodile rolls in the water when it catches its prey. When nothing happened she examined the wire again and clamping her teeth on it once more began turning her body in the other direction. This time when she came to a stop and opened her jaws, the two ends of the wire sprang apart.

Fang immediately hopped in, caught the wire with his two long front teeth and pulled it out of the catch. As he did so, the door of the cage swung open.

'Come on Snowflake,' he whispered. 'You're free.' When she didn't move, he added, 'Nightshade and Bluebell are waiting for you. Come on. Hurry!'

The mention of her two friends seemed to remind Snowflake of the night the doors of their cages at the fur farm had been flung open, and she got up.

'Hurry,' urged Black Tip, 'before the dogs come back – or the trapper. Remember what he did to you in the yard.'

Snowflake bounded out of the cage and followed them through the hole in the side of the barn. They kept running until they reached the cover of the hedge and when they stopped, Fang endeavoured to thank the badger.

However, the badger would have none of it. 'It was no

trouble at all,' she protested.

'You can at least return to your family with something to eat,' said Snowflake. So saying, she ran over to the truck, jumped up on to the back and returned with a dead chicken which she dropped at the badger's feet. 'And there's another one up there,' she added, a look of triumph in her eyes.

When Snowflake returned with the other chicken, Fang said, 'The trapper must have brought them along for bait. He took one with him.'

'Well, these two are ours,' she announced. 'One for us, and one for our friend who was good enough to come and help us.'

The badger smiled. 'I appreciate your offer Snowflake, but to tell you the truth, beetles and worms are more to my liking.'

Seeing that Snowflake was somewhat crestfallen, the badger added, 'But, I'll take one back for your friends if you like'

'And I'll take the other one back,' said Black Tip.

With that the badger galloped away, the chicken flapping wildly from the side of her mouth.

'Better go after her,' said Fang. 'Her teeth may be better than ours, but not her eyes. Make sure she doesn't run into a trap.'

Black Tip made to go, but paused. 'Aren't you coming too?'

Fang shook his head. 'There are too many of us. Old Sage Brush said so himself. You'll have a better chance of reaching the Hills of the Long Low Cloud if you're fewer in number.'

Black Tip smiled. 'Are you sure?'

Fang nodded. 'I'm sure.'

'All right. Come on Snowflake. Time we were going.'

Snowflake hung back. 'Fang and I were talking – you know, when we were waiting for you and the badger. I told him that if I got free I would go with him.'

Black Tip smiled again. 'Okay, if that's what you want. But take care, both of you. The trapper's still out there some-where and he won't be pleased when he finds his lovely snowflake has melted away!'

Nothing more was said and they went their separate ways – Black Tip to rejoin Old Sage Brush and the others on their journey to the Hills of the Long Low Cloud, Fang and Snowflake to journey somewhere else where they could make a new life for themselves.

★ ★ ★

If the magpies saw Black Tip and the badger racing back to the sett with the chickens dangling from their mouths, they didn't follow them. Instead they decided more fun was to be had with Fang who was limping slowly along the side of a field.

Fang lay down and looked up at them. Something Black Tip had said had given him an idea. The trapper, Black Tip had said, would not be happy when he found that his lovely snowflake had melted away.

A short distance farther on Fang lay down again, this time on a patch of snow on the side of the hedge where the sun had not yet reached. The magpies had followed him and it wasn't long before they began mobbing him. When they came too close, he put up a paw in what seemed a very weak movement to ward them off. Thinking that perhaps he was injured or dying, the biggest and most daring of the magpies landed closer to him, but just out of range. Fang still didn't move, and the same magpie landed again, this time even closer and ventured to peck at his tail. However, it had failed to see a second fox lying nearby because it was white and, like the other snowflakes, had melted into the snow.

Snowflake pounced and grabbed the magpie. The other magpies immediately scattered and flew to a more distant hedge where they flicked their tails to keep their balance as they tried to comprehend what had happened to their leader.

Ignoring them, Fang and Snowflake made their way into the depths of the hedge where they stripped the dead magpie of its feathers and settled down to a well-earned meal. As they munched away, they smiled at one another and recalled how they had fooled the biggest flithengibber of them all.

'It was your idea,' Snowflake conceded.

'Maybe so,' Fang said, 'but I couldn't have done it without you.'

'And Old Sage Brush was right,' Snowflake added. 'It doesn't matter if the paw is black or white so long as it can catch a mouse.'

Fang smiled. 'Or a magpie!'

It was a trophy they both savoured and a story, they knew, Old Sage Brush would enjoy if ever they met him again. It was also a story they would some day tell to their cubs.

NINE

Hop-along's Nightmare

In the Mound of the Badgers, the foxes dined on the chickens as Black Tip recounted how cruelly the trapper had treated Snowflake and how the mother badger had managed to free her.

'And the trapper left you two chickens!' Old Sage Brush chuckled. 'That was very kind of him.'

'You can laugh now,' said Black Tip, 'but it was no laughing matter at the time.'

'It's the thought of the trapper losing his white fox – and his chickens – that I find amusing,' said the old fox. 'I can just imagine what it was like for all of you. You did very well.'

'It was Fang's idea to get the badger,' Black Tip added.

'Otherwise we could never have freed Snowflake.'

'But now she's gone,' Bluebell lamented. 'Nightshade and I will miss her.'

'Fang will look after her,' Vickey assured her. 'He's a fine strong fox. And who knows, maybe we'll meet up with them again.'

'I hope so,' said Nightshade.

'I wonder if the others who escaped from the cages were captured or... maybe even...' Bluebell couldn't bring herself to say the word killed.

'Others may have survived too,' suggested She-la.

'When we get to the Hills of the Long Low Cloud, you'll be safe,' said Vickey, 'and who knows what colour of foxes we will meet along the way.'

Hop-along, who was lying nearby listened, but said nothing. They hadn't reached the stage where they could even see the Hills of the Long Low Cloud, and to make matters worse the trapper was on their trail. Fang and Snowflake had gone their own way, but there were still too many of them left. Even if they travelled alone they couldn't hide their tracks from the trapper.

When the others had finished eating, they began to doze, but Hop-along began to think and the more he thought about it, the more he realised the Hills of the Long Low Cloud were too far away, especially for him. Even if he did manage to reach them, how would he make it back? His faith in Old Sage Brush had been restored, but the truth was he lacked the faith in himself to go much farther. The trapper had left him with only three legs – and his dreams. He had dreamt of nights when his cunning had made up for his handicap and he had done feats no other fox could do. He had also dreamt that his paw was back and he had four fine legs again, fleet of foot and able to outrun every danger.

Dreams, however, were for when he was asleep. The nightmare came when he was awake. When he looked at the place where his paw should be, he knew he could do very little. That was when the reality of his situation sank in. He couldn't even hunt for himself. For most of the time he was dependent upon others, especially his mate, She-la. And now the man who had deprived him of his paw was back.

When they began to stir from their slumber, Hop-along said, 'He's still out there.'

'Who?' asked Old Sage Brush.

'The trapper.'

The old fox nodded. He had tried to lighten their hearts by laughing at the trapper's loss and celebrating their gains. 'I know, I know,' he said, for in truth he could think of nothing more to say.

Hop-along got up and hobbled into one of the side chambers where he could be alone with his thoughts.

'He's right you know,' said Black Tip. 'Fang saw the trapper leave the farm. But he wasn't going away. He was going out to set more traps.'

'Are you sure he didn't come this way?' asked She-la.

'Of course I am. If he had come this way the badger and myself would have run straight into him.'

'He must have seen Snowflake's tracks coming from the mound,' said Vickey.

'And ours,' added Black Tip. 'So he must know we are all here.'

'That mean's we're trapped,' said She-la.

Old Sage Brush nodded. 'In a way we are trapped, but I think there is a way we can get out.'

'You mean by a rear exit?' asked Black Tip. 'We can't. There's still snow on the ground. We would leave too many tracks.'

The old fox shook his head. 'That's not what I had in mind.' He paused. 'The trapper is very smart, so we must be smarter. He knows we are in here – but we know he is out there. That means we must stay here long enough to make him think we've left.'

'And how will we know he has left?' asked Hop-along.

'It will be a waiting game,' Old Sage Brush told him. 'He will make his move and we will make ours – but not until we are ready.'

When a fox is injured it can lie up without food for days, even weeks in man's time, until it has recovered and is able to hunt again. This Old Sage Brush and his group now determined to do in an effort to outwit the trapper. They curled up close to one another for warmth and slept. When they weren't sleeping they talked. And when they talked, Bluebell and Nightshade heard stories of other journeys the old fox and his friends had made, of new friends they had met along the way – foxes, badgers and even an otter –and of the dangers they had overcome.

They listened in disbelief as the red foxes told them of the strange animals they had seen in Man's Place – some with noses so long they touched the ground, others with necks so long they could nibble leaves on the trees without even stretching, giant ginger cats that were fed huge chunks of meat by man and exotic birds that the foxes had dared to catch for themselves.

As time passed, there was no night, no day, just the darkness of the sett. More stories were told, and Bluebell and Nightshade were thrilled to hear how one of their friends had once rescued a vixen from the howling dogs.

'Skulking Dog,' Black Tip recalled. 'But he couldn't have done it without the help of another little fox we met along the way.'

'Running Fox,' said Vickey. 'He was very brave. Not a bit afraid of the howling dogs. Or if he was, he didn't show it. We called our little vixen after him.'

'What are the howling dogs like?' asked Bluebell. 'We've never seen them.'

'With luck you'll hear them long before you see them,' said Black Tip. 'They're big and fast and man brings them out in great numbers to hunt us.'

'He rides behind them on his horse,' Vickey explained. 'They won't give up and we have to use every trick we know to get away from them.'

'Maybe you could teach us some of those tricks,' said Nightshade.

'We will,' Old Sage Brush told them, 'but all in good time,'

There was no better teacher than the old fox. He had taught the other red foxes many things and now as they whiled away the time in the darkness of the Mound of the Badgers, he taught Bluebell and Nightshade many things.

'Snowflake told us she forgot what you said about learning from the heron,' said Black Tip. 'She said she was sorry, but got so excited at the sight of the snow that she just galloped down the field and into the trapper's net.'

'The problem,' the old fox told Bluebell and Nightshade, 'is that when you're sorry you didn't do something it is usually too late. What I told you about the heron was just one example of what you can learn from the other creatures around you. The thrush, for instance, runs a little then stops. Stop and go, stop and go, all the while looking for worms and listening for man. Or when it cocks its head to one side, perhaps it is listening for worms and looking for man. Either way, it is something you must do – keep an ear to the ground and an eye out for danger, or an eye on your quarry and an ear cocked for man. That way you will not be caught unawares.

Before being forced to stay underground, Bluebell and Nightshade had noticed that the thrushes and blackbirds would be out early each morning looking for worms and snails.

'The thrushes with the speckled breasts and the black birds with the yellow beaks are always with us,' Old Sage Brush continued, 'but some birds only come when it suits them. The swallows come when it's warm. Others come when it's cold, like the thrushes with the red wings and, of course, the geese with the black heads.'

'Geese!' exclaimed Nightshade. 'You mean like the one Hop-along caught in the Field of the Thistles?'

The old fox chuckled. 'No, no. They're big white geese. They just waddle around the farmyards. The geese I'm talking about are small and dark and they fly.'

'They follow their leader,' Vickey explained, 'flying in the shape of a fox's nose.'

'Like the ripples an otter leaves as it swims in the lake,' added Black Tip.

'Quite so,' agreed the old fox.

'You're thinking of Whiskers,' said Vickey.

'Of course,' said her mate. 'He was a great friend.'

Turning to Bluebell and Nightshade, Vickey told them,

'Whiskers was the otter we were telling you about. We met him on our first journey.'

'He also took us on our great journey to the edge of the world,' said Black Tip.

Bluebell shivered. 'Oh, I don't know if I would like to see that.'

'You still have a lot to learn and a lot to see,' said the old fox. 'Now, the geese I was telling you about. They come in to feed in the fields.'

'Like the red-winged thrushes, they arrive in flocks,' added Black Tip.

'They don't really have red wings,' Vickey corrected him. 'It's the feathers underneath the wings that are red.'

'It matters not,' said the old fox. 'It's the geese I am talking about. When they come it will be time for us to go.'

'Why?' asked Bluebell.

'Why what?'

'Why will it be time for us to go?'

'Because,' explained the old fox, 'the geese come in great numbers and when they walk around in search of food it will tell us that our paths through the fields are free of traps – or at least some of them.'

'How do you know they will come to feed in these fields?' asked Nightshade.

Old Sage Brush sighed, but endeavoured to be patient. 'Fang told me that he used to hunt in these fields and he saw them for himself. When I had my sight, I also saw them, and I noted that for some strange reason they came back to the same fields to feed.'

How long the foxes stayed in the Mound of the Badgers, they themselves did not know, for much of the time they slept to conserve energy. When they were awake and the stories of cunning had been exhausted, the old fox told stories of great hunting trips he had been told when he was young. In describing what had been caught, he would weave a feast that filled their minds with food and their stomachs with promise, and in doing so help placate their hunger. Nevertheless, the hunger pains were never far away, and sometimes it seemed the geese would never come. But Old Sage Brush had said they would come and come they did.

It was Black Tip who spotted them first. He had been taking turns with Vickey and She-la to watch for them at the entrance to the sett, and rushed back in shouting, 'They're here. They're here.'

The others hurried out to the entrance. The snow had gone, and something much more exciting was about to fall. Looking up, they saw lines of geese following their leader as they wheeled in over the mound before settling in the fields below. Many more followed and Old Sage Brush, chuckled. He didn't need to see them. He could hear them. Making his way out past the others, he said, 'It's time to go.'

The rest of them needed no bidding. They were lean now

from their enforced fast but the old fox warned them to take their time. Whatever about the fields, he told them, the hedgerows could still hold danger. Somehow they resisted the temptation to run and cautiously made their way down to the fields.

Suddenly, Bluebell stopped, saying, 'I hear dogs barking.'

'That's not dogs,' the old fox told her. 'That's the sound the geese make when they're feeding.'

The others laughed, but the old fox reproached them, saying, 'How are they to know what they've heard if they haven't heard it before?'

Black Tip nodded. 'And how are they to know what these geese taste like unless we catch them.'

To their delight, Bluebell and Nightshade found that the first field they came to contained many of the geese. They were small and dark, just as the old fox had described them, and they were walking around, honking and barking and pecking at the grass.

'How are we going to catch them?' Nightshade asked Black Tip.

'They're strange birds,' he replied. 'Ducks take to the air as soon as we approach them, but these geese don't take flight. They just walk away from us.'

'And that's how we'll catch them,' said Vickey.

When the others had circled around and concealed them-selves in the farthest hedge, Vickey and Bluebell trotted into the field. The geese moved away from them but didn't take flight. They continued slowly across the field and again the geese moved away from them. They then criss-crossed the field and the geese moved towards the hedge. Some of the geese were now glancing nervously at the two of them but were unaware that other foxes lay in wait.

As the geese edged closer and closer to the hedge, Old Sage Brush and Hop-along listened while the others watched. When they judged the geese were close enough, Black Tip, She-la and Nightshade pounced on three of them. Only then did the other geese take to the air, not in a tidy formation, but in a disorganised, noisy flock. They circled around the area a couple of times before landing in a nearby field, but the foxes didn't go to see which one. It was so long since they had eaten they didn't stop until the dark brown and white feathers of their catch were the only things left.

Flocks of thrushes with grey heads and reddish feathers were now coming in, but the foxes didn't try to catch any of them. They were too small and took flight easily, and anyway, it was time to move on.

As Old Sage Brush had predicted, the geese had walked the fields for them and showed that the trapper had not put down any of his snapping jaws in their path. Nor did they come across any of his nets or choking hedge-traps, and so they pressed on, confident that they had left the trapper behind.

It wasn't until they came to a narrow strip of marshy land covered with sally bushes and tussocks of withered grass that they realised their mistake.

Black Tip was leading the way along a path that had been used by other foxes, when he came across something lying beside a low, round boulder.

'What is it?' asked Old Sage Brush who was trotting along behind him.

'The head of a chicken,' Black Tip replied, ' but I think it may be a trap.'

'What makes you think that?'

'Fang said he saw the trapper taking a dead chicken with him when he went up the fields with his traps.'

Having heard what Black Tip had said, Hop-along hobbled up to him. The head of the chicken, he could see, was lying on withered grass that had been pulled and scattered on the path. He had seen the trapper's handiwork before and knew immediately that Black Tip's suspicions were well-founded. 'Don't move – any of you,' he cautioned. 'Don't move.' He bent down, picked up a small stone and dropped it onto the chicken's head. The jaws of a metal trap that was hidden underneath immediately sprang shut.

Bluebell and Nightshade jumped with fright and turned, ready to run, but She-la warned them to stay still.

'Don't step off the path,' Hop-along called back. 'In fact, don't take another step. There may be others.'

Acutely aware that none of them knew more about the snapping jaws than Hop-along, the others waited as he hobbled here and there, examining the ground with great care before every step.

'There are more,' he said. 'Up ahead and on each side.'

'Then we must go back the way we came,' said the old fox.

'We can't,' Black Tip told him. 'Bluebell and Nightshade are behind us. They're scared and edgy and if we try to turn them around who knows what they'll do.'

'Okay,' said Hop-along. 'Everyone lie down and stay calm. I'll try and find a way through.'

'Be careful,' cried She-la.

'Just talk to Bluebell and Nightshade,' Hop-along called back. 'Make sure they don't move – don't any of you move.'

Black Tip lay down and the others followed suit. They said nothing, but as Hop-along hobbled forward they feared that if he didn't spot one of the snapping jaws and stepped on it, he would lose another leg. Now and then he stopped to pick up a small branch or a stone and when he dropped it, there was a clash of metal as the steel jaws snapped shut. With each snap of the jaws, Bluebell and Nightshade made to get up, and it was all Vickey and She-la could do to calm them and keep them from running into some of the other traps that had been laid for them.

★ ★ ★

The trapper had chosen the place for his traps well. He had seen new tracks coming from and going to the badger sett, but knew that after netting the white fox the others would be on the alert and not as easy to catch. He was also angered by the discovery that the white one had escaped, so he had decided that instead of nets he would put down traps. Dead or alive, injured or not, he reckoned the coloured foxes would still be worth good money.

It seemed that the foxes were still going in a particular direction, perhaps in search of a new territory, and the question was where to lay his traps. Every winter he had seen Brent geese arriving from Greenland and Canada to feed in the fields not far from the mound. What they fed on he didn't know, but he knew they would be coming back again soon. Redwings and field fares would also be arriving from Scandinavia to search for worms and berries. With disturbance like that there was no point in putting traps there.

Some distance farther on was a small valley that lay between two farms and he thought it was likely the foxes would pass through that. On one side of the valley was a large sloping field on which the farmer had sown winter wheat that would ripen in summer. On the other side were bare rolling fields belonging to the sheep farmer in whose barn he had stored his traps and from which the white fox had escaped.

As the foxes were moving in a group he knew they would want to use whatever cover they could find rather than cross open ground. As a result he had laid several of his metal traps among grassy tussocks and sallies in a narrow strip of scrub land that lay between the two farms. The gin traps, as they were known, were illegal – but who was to see them? He smiled. Hopefully not the foxes.

* * *

Hop-along now endeavoured to lead his friends through what would become known to them as the Field of the Snapping Jaws. It was slow, tedious and very dangerous and the others watched with bated breath as, bit by bit, he moved farther ahead of them. With each faltering step, each clang of the metal, they feared that an agonising scream would tell them he was a prisoner of the trapper once more. It was an agonising wait and as it continued, they also feared that the trapper would come upon them. If that happened and they were forced to scatter, they would all be caught.

At long last, however, Hop-along turned and called back to them that the way was clear. When they joined him he put the stump of his leg on top of one of the traps he had sprung, telling Bluebell and Nightshade, 'This is what you must look out for.'

The two of them cringed, Bluebell saying, 'Oh no. You've

caught your leg in it!'

'Of course I haven't caught my leg in it,' he said. 'That's what happened to me a long time ago.' He removed the stump of his leg and they could see that the half moon-shaped metal jaws were already closed. 'I just wanted to show you what will happen to you if you don't look where you're going.'

When they had reached firmer ground, Old Sage Brush stopped, saying, 'You've done well Hop-along. Had it not been for you we might have lost much more than a paw. Now, we'd better be on our way before the trapper comes back to check his traps.'

Hop-along hung back. 'Sorry Sage Brush, but I'm afraid this is as far as I go.'

'We've been talking,' said She-la, 'and we've decided it's time we returned to the Land of Sinna.'

'The truth is,' Hop-along explained, 'I can't go on.'

Old Sage Brush nodded. 'That's okay. I understand.'

'We all do,' added Vickey. 'We know how difficult it's been for you.'

'Perhaps you should keep to the open fields,' Black Tip told him. 'They might be safer than the one we've just come through. And the trapper won't be looking for you out there.'

Hop-along smiled. 'Don't worry about me. I've my own plans for the trapper.'

With that they parted company, but instead of heading for

the open fields, Hop-along and She-la retraced their steps through the Field of the Snapping Jaws. There they stopped at the low, round boulder where Hop-along had sprung the trap on which the trapper had left the chicken's head as bait.

'Wait here,' he told She-la.

Before re-entering the field, Hop-along had outlined his plan to She-la and she now watched nervously as he went in off the path and looked around for a trap that had not been sprung.

'This should do it,' he said at last.

She-la didn't want to discourage her mate. At the same time she didn't want him to put himself in danger. 'I hope it works,' she said.

Hop-along smiled. 'Don't worry. It'll work.'

'What if the trapper has his dog with him?'

'He didn't have it when he netted Snowflake, and he'll hardly bring it to a field with so many traps lying around. So stop worrying.'

The idea for what Hop-along was going to do had come to him when he had put his paw on top of the snapping jaws and Bluebell and Nightshade thought he had been caught in it. She-la had to admit that it was an audacious plan. She realised that if it worked it might help her mate put to rest the nightmare he had suffered since the trapper had deprived him of his paw. However, she also knew that if it didn't work, it could cost him his life.

It was, therefore, with the greatest of misgivings that She-la agreed to take part. As they moved to put the plan into action, she hid behind one of the large tussocks of grass just in off the path, while Hop-along lay down beside the rock near to where he had dropped the stone to spring the first trap.

Unaware that two of the foxes had laid a trap of their own, the trapper approached the strip of scrub land. His cigarette smoke, wafting in the wind, alerted She-la, then Hop-along to his impending arrival. She-la squeezed herself down as low as she could, but not Hop-along. He got up and put the stump of his paw on top of the trap. At the same time he began to writhe and scream in agony.

Seeing a fox that appeared to be caught in one of his traps, the trapper moved forward, taking care to avoid other traps he had laid in the area. As he approached the rock, She-la dashed out of her hiding place and ran off along the path. Taken by surprise, the trapper stumbled off the path. In doing so he stepped on one of his own traps and the metal jaws snapped shut on his ankle, just above his boots. The sharp teeth dug deeply into his shin bone and he yelled out in pain. Hopping around on the other leg, he grabbed the trap with both hands in a futile effort to try and open it. In his pain he forgot that the trap was tied to a wire that he had pegged securely to the ground. When the wire went taught, he stumbled and fell. He had a fleeting glimpse of the fox taking the stump of its leg off the other trap before he hit his head on the rock and blacked out.

When She-la looked around she saw her mate standing beside the inert body of the trapper. Afraid to venture any nearer, she asked, 'Is he dead?'

Hop-along was staring at the paw around the trapper's neck. 'I don't know.'

'Come on,' she panted. 'We'd better get out of here.'

'Not before I get this.' Reaching forward, Hop-along grabbed his paw and yanked it with all the force he could muster. The leather thong that had held it around the trapper's neck for so long broke. Hop-along pulled it away and as he hobbled after She-la, he smiled. The paw was in his mouth, not on his leg, but it didn't matter. Somehow he felt complete again, a four-legged fox in all but name.

TEN

THE FOREST OF FEAR

Three of the foxes fixed their eyes on the night sky in the hope of seeing the flashing tails of those who had crossed over to the afterlife, but saw none. However, the moon didn't seem at all concerned. It was smiling down at them as if amused at their efforts to spot the shooting stars.

'We couldn't see the wide eye of gloomglow from our cages,' Bluebell recalled. 'Or the flashing tails.'

'When the days are longer and the nights are shorter,' Vickey told them, 'you will see many things that you could not see from your cages.'.'

'Like what?' asked Bluebell.

'Well, like bats.'

'Bats?' said Nightshade. 'What are they?'

'They're like mice, only they have wings.'

Nightshade and Bluebell laughed, Bluebell saying, 'Flying mice? We do have a lot to learn.'

'They come out as darkness falls,' Vickey continued. 'You'll see them flitting across the wide eye of gloomglow.'

'And why can't we see them now?' asked Nightshade.

'Because they don't seem to come out when it's cold. And that's another thing. We've seen them in old buildings and in caves. They sleep hanging upside down from the roof.'

The other two laughed again and looked up at the wide eye of gloomglow. It was still smiling and they wondered if it also smiled at the bats.

Unlike man, Vickey and her friends had no superstition about the bat. It didn't bother them, and they didn't bother it. The fact was they couldn't, as it was always beyond their reach. In a way they actually admired the bat. Their eyesight being much superior to man's, they could see the bat catching insects on the wing. This they considered to be a great feat, equalled only by the swallow and the swift in their continual hunt for food.

Had the foxes known that man secretly feared the bat, they might have wondered why, just as they wondered why he sometimes feared the cry of the vixen. The reason for that was not apparent to them any more than the reason why Ratwiddle was able to make his predictions. Man's reaction to their cries had come as a great surprise to all of them, with the exception of Old Sage Brush. But, just as Ratwiddle had predicted, man had feared the fox.

How the fox could hunt the man, they couldn't imagine. Then, as they continued their journey, the cry of another vixen gave them the news that the trapper had been caught in his own trap. The cry was taken up and relayed by other vixens, and as the news spread there was great rejoicing in the fox world.

Vickey smiled. 'They say it was Hop-along's doing.'

'I wouldn't be surprised,' said Black Tip. 'But I can't think how.'

The foxes that followed Old Sage Brush would learn no more of the trapper's fate until they returned to the Land of Sinna. When that time came, She-la would tell them how her mate, their faithful friend Hop-along, had got revenge on his arch enemy by luring him into the trap. Only then would they realise that Ratwiddle's second prediction had come true, and that the fox had hunted the man.

Man, however, is only one of the enemies of the creatures of the wild, as many of them hunt one another. The mouse hunts the beetle, the rat hunts the mouse, the cat hunts the rat and the dog hunts the cat. Many of them are hunted by the fox which, in turn, is hunted by the hound.

These things, Bluebell and Nightshade learned as they journeyed on towards the Hills of the Long Low Cloud. Soon they would learn of other creatures that hunted, and were hunted, in what they would come to know as the

Forest of Fear.

Having travelled some distance, the foxes found themselves in a small pine forest. Such a forest, Bluebell and Nightshade discovered, was of no use to a fox. The ground was covered with pine needles and there wasn't so much as a blade of grass to feed a rabbit or hide a hare. Not that it mattered. The scent of pine was so strong they could smell nothing else. The only creature that could survive in a place like this, they were told, was the squirrel. Strangely, the pine cones were intact. Not one of them had been nibbled by a squirrel.

'Well, pine cones are no good to us,' said Old Sage Brush, so they pressed on until they came to a larger forest beside a lake. It consisted of oak, ash, beech, sycamore, chestnut, hazel and birch, all broad-leaved trees, although the leaves had now gone. On the edge of the forest they found an unoccupied earth and as the group was fewer in number now, it was able to accommodate them all.

As they settled in they could see that whatever fox had dug the earth had chosen well. It was dry and the entrance was hidden by a thick tangle of hedging. Yet there was no sign that it had been used recently and they concluded that it had been abandoned for some time. However, it wasn't until an otter peered into it that they discovered why.

'Whiskers!' Vickey exclaimed. 'Is that you?'

The otter smiled. 'Who else would dare poke his nose into a fox earth?'

It was coming on to dusk and Black Tip followed Vickey outside to greet their old friend. They also introduced him to Bluebell and Nightshade.

'Blue, black, silver,' said Whiskers. 'Not white I hope.'

'Why not?' asked Bluebell defensively. 'Much of my fur is white underneath.'

'And our friend Snowflake is white,' added Nightshade.

'I didn't mean to offend you,' Whiskers explained. 'It's just that white has become a problem for me – and for others who live here.'

Hearing a voice that was familiar to him but one he hadn't heard in a long time, Old Sage Brush emerged from the earth and cocking an ear, said, 'Whiskers?'

'If you could swim as well as you can hear, you would make a fine otter,' Whiskers told him.

The old fox smiled. 'If you could hear as well as you can swim, you would make a fine fox!' The others laughed and he asked, 'What do you mean, when you say white has become a problem for you?'

'The lake has been invaded by mink – white mink.'

'I have never seen white mink,' said Vickey.'

'And I have never seen a white fox,' Whiskers responded, 'or a blue one – until now.'

'They must be the mink that escaped from the fur farm,' Bluebell told him.

'White mink, blue foxes,' said Whiskers. 'Tell me about this fur farm so that I may understand why these creatures have come to fish in my lake.'

Between them, Bluebell and Nightshade told him about the night the shadowy figures had broken into the fur farm and set them free.

'We didn't know what to do when the cages were opened,' recalled Bluebell. 'Then we saw the mink streaming out through the hole in the fence and Nightshade said we should go too.'

'There were many more mink than foxes in the cages,' Nightshade added.

Whiskers nodded. 'They must have come up the river and streams. That's why they got here before you.'

'So their arrival has caused you a problem,' said the old fox.

Whiskers sat back on his hind legs. 'A big problem – and not only for me. The brown mink who were already here aren't very pleased about it either.'

'You mean too many mink and not enough fish?'

'Not enough of anything. Fish, eels, waterhens, coots, ducks, you name it. The white mink have cleared the lot.'

'How did they know how to hunt?' asked Bluebell. 'Our friends have had to show us how.'

'And we're still learning,' said Nightshade.

'I don't think the white mink had anything to learn,' Whiskers told her. 'Or if they did, it didn't take them long. They're going mad out there. The brown mink can't keep up with them. Neither can I. There are just too many of them.'

'But isn't the mink a relative of yours?' said Vickey.

Whiskers nodded. 'It is, but it makes no difference.'

'So what are you going to do?' asked Black Tip.

'Find another lake – before they do!'

'Pity you have to go,' said Black Tip. 'At least we'll have the forest to hunt in.'

'The forest is not a happy place either, as you'll discover.'

'Why not?' asked the old fox.

'Because another relative of the mink has taken it over.'

'A relative of the mink!' said Vickey. 'Then it must be a relative of yours.'

'It is, but I don't climb trees – it does. Which reminds me. I met a friend of yours the other day – the one with his paws on the ground and his mind in the sky.'

'You mean, Ratwiddle?' exclaimed Vickey. 'What was he doing here?'

Whiskers shook his head. 'Your friend doesn't speak as you do.'

'Tell me about it,' grumbled Black Tip.

'He just said, "You don't have to climb trees to catch fish."'

'What a strange thing to say,' added Vickey.

'I thought it was a silly thing to say,' said Whiskers. 'I mean, nobody knows more about catching fish than otters – apart from mink, of course. And everyone knows we don't have to climb trees to get them.'

'Ratwiddle may be strange.' said the old fox. 'Silly he is not. I can see many things in my mind's eye, and he can see farther. But tell me, which relative of yours hunts in the forest? The stoat perhaps?'

'No. A much more fearsome hunter than the stoat. In our branch of the family we call it the tree cat.'

Old Sage Brush nodded. 'A fearsome hunter indeed. Fox-lore speaks highly of its prowess.'

'Our stories too,' said Whiskers. 'It seems the tree cat has always been with us – but not the mink. Our stories only speak of the times when the mink escaped from fur farms and caused the kind of problems we are having now.'

What Whiskers had spoken of as the tree cat, is known in much of man's world as the pine marten or the marten cat. Only in Gaelic – *cat crainn* – does he call it the tree cat, and for good reason. It's an excellent climber, coming down trees at great speed to seize squirrels, mice or small birds and darting back up again to devour its prey out of sight among the upper branches.

'One tree cat shouldn't be a problem,' said Black Tip. 'There should be plenty for all of us.'

'But there's more than one of them,' Whiskers told him. 'They've come to hunt the squirrel – and anything else they can find – and they don't like outsiders.'

'We saw no squirrels in the pine forest,' Vickey recalled.

'That's because there are no more left in it. Red squirrels

used to live there, but the tree cats cleaned them out. Now they've come to this forest to hunt the grey squirrels – and red ones if they can find them.'

'Still,' said Black Tip, 'there should be enough to go round.'

'You would think so,' said Whiskers, 'and indeed that used to be the case. This was a very peaceful place. A lake where I could hunt as I pleased. Woods where I could take a fish and eat it at my leisure. But things have changed. Now the brown mink fight with the white mink. The grey squirrels fight with the red squirrels. And the tree cats fight with them all.' He sighed. 'I'm afraid my relatives have laid waste to the lake and turned the woods into a forest of fear.'

Old Sage Brush nodded. 'I'm sorry to hear that. I know how much you enjoy the river and the lakes and, of course, the woods.'

There was silence as they all reflected on what the otter had said.

'I have often spoken to my younger friends about the importance of the balance of nature,' the old fox continued. 'Too many creatures of one kind, too few of another can upset the balance. When that happens, things can go badly wrong. From what you say, it appears to me that is what has happened here. Too many grey squirrels, too few reds, too many white mink, too few fish.'

'And not enough for the likes of me,' added Whiskers.

'The question is, how can we can we bring the situation

back into balance?' said the old fox.

'We?' asked Black Tip. 'How can we do anything about it, and why should we? It's not our problem.'

'No, but it is a problem for our friend Whiskers, and if there's not enough food to go around it also becomes our problem.'

'But we don't eat squirrels or fish,' argued Black Tip. 'I know we would if we could, but we can't catch them'

'True,' said the old fox, 'but mink eat much more than fish.'

Whiskers nodded. 'They also eat frogs, rats, chickens, ducks, rabbits, anything they can find.'

'And some of that should be there for us,' the old fox added.

'But squirrels don't take any of our food,' said Black Tip. 'They just eat nuts.'

'I know,' Whiskers said, 'but it's because of the squirrels that the tree cats are there and they are like mink. They eat anything they can find. Both, I'm afraid, have left precious little for us.'

Vickey, who had listened patiently to the discussion, asked, 'So what can we do about it?'

'I don't know,' the old fox confessed, 'but I suspect Ratwiddle may have been trying to give us the answer. Remind me, Whiskers. What was it he said?'

'He said you don' have to climb trees to catch fish.'

'I wonder what he meant?' said Vickey.

Black Tip cast his eyes up to the heavens that Ratwiddle always seemed to be looking at, saying, 'You know him.'

'Black Tip,' said the old fox, 'why don't you go into the forest and see what you can find. Take Bluebell and Nightshade with you.'

'But they're not…' Black Tip began. 'They're not experienced enough.'

'One is black, the other white,' the old fox countered. 'Maybe they can talk to the mink, be they black or white, whichever you encounter.'

Black Tip was about to say that any mink he had seen were dark brown not black and Bluebell was blue, but decided against it. Maybe some mink were black, and Bluebell's under fur was white. Anyway, the old fox had obviously made up his mind, and he reckoned there was nothing he could do or say to change it.

'I'll show them the way,' said Whiskers. 'It isn't in the nature of the tree cat to stop and talk. But perhaps the mink will talk to them.'

'And if they don't,' the old fox said, 'maybe they'll talk to you – seeing as how you're related.'

Whiskers smiled, but didn't reply. The old fox, he could see, was older than when he first met him but as wily as ever. However, he added, 'Perhaps it might be best if they waited until daylight.'

'Why?' asked Black Tip. 'Night is our best time for hunting. I imagine we can see better than any of them in the dark.'

'Maybe so,' Whiskers told him. 'But believe me you don't want to go in there in the dark.'

Whatever about Black Tip, Bluebell and Nightshade were more than happy to wait until daylight. For when darkness closed in around them, much squealing and screaming could be heard coming from the direction of the trees and the lake shore. So much so that even when daylight came, it was with great trepidation that they set off with Black Tip and Whiskers to enter what the otter had called the Forest of Fear.

As they approached the trees, Black Tip said, 'I wonder what Ratwiddle meant when he said you don't have to climb trees to catch fish?'

'You tell me,' Whiskers replied. 'He's one of your kind, not mine.'

'Maybe,' said Nightshade, 'he meant that if we look hard enough, we don't have to climb trees to get the answer.'

Bluebell stopped and looked at her. 'That's very good Nightshade.'

The answer to their problem, however, was not very obvious, no matter how hard they looked. The first squirrel they came across was red and it was dead. It was horribly disfigured and reminded Black Tip of the way rabbits used to look when they got the sleeping sickness.

As they wondered what had happened to it, a voice from

above said, 'It's the scourge.'

Looking up, they found that the speaker was another red squirrel. Its underside was a creamy white and as it shifted its position, they saw its tail was curled back up over its head.

'It's the scourge of the greys,' the squirrel continued. 'The tree cat drove us from the pine forest where we lived on cones. Here we have to live on nuts, but the greys eat them before they are ripe, something we cannot do. And because there are so many of them, they find the nuts we bury before we can find them.'

'You mean your friend died of hunger?' asked Black Tip.

'No. I told you. It's the scourge of the greys. When we get it, it kills us, especially when we are weak with hunger.'

'So it kills the greys too?' said Bluebell.

'No!' was the squirrel's surprising answer. 'They don't seem to suffer from it at all.'

'Then how can you call it the scourge of the greys?' asked Nightshade.

'Because we never suffered from it until they came.'

The foxes found this difficult to understand but weren't in a position to argue the point.

'Are there many of you left here?' asked Bluebell.

'Only me and my mate. We're the last of the reds.'

Farther into the forest, they came across several grey squirrels searching for food at the base of a tree. Black Tip was about to speak to them when, without warning a tree cat descended upon them, grabbed one and sped back up the tree. The rest of the squirrels immediately sped up some nearby trees and in an instant the clearing was deserted.

'No hope of talking to them,' said Black Tip.

Whiskers agreed. 'It'll be a while before they come down again, and as I said before, the tree cat doesn't stop to ask questions – or answer them!'

The shrubbery on the rocky shoreline, they discovered, was full of mink. Peering eyes here, a snout there, a rustle, a splash, a squeak.

'Maybe they'll recognise my scent,' whispered Bluebell, 'and know I came from the same farm as they did.'

'And mine,' added Nightshade.

Before Whiskers or Black Tip could stop her, Bluebell took a few tentative steps towards the shrubbery. However, all the white mink recognised was another creature coming to compete for the little food that was left in the lake. Several of them sprang upon her and grabbed her by the neck and it was only because of the swift intervention of Whiskers and Black Tip that more didn't leap upon her.

Many more mink were poking their snouts out of the undergrowth now, squeaking and hissing in a most threatening manner and as Whiskers tore the attackers from Bluebell's neck, Nightshade stepped forward to confront the others. Fearing that she would suffer a similar attack, Black Tip jumped in to protect her, throwing the nearest mink into the water. Strangely, though, none of them attacked her.

'Run!' Whiskers shouted. 'All of you. I'll try and hold them back.'

As the foxes turned and raced through the trees, they could hear fearful squeaks and screams coming from the lake. They didn't like leaving Whiskers, but they knew he was better able to cope with the mink than they were. When they arrived at the clearing they stopped, determined to help if the mink pursued him. By this time, parts of Bluebell's fur were beginning to take on another colour as spots of blood oozed out of the bites on her neck.

'Are you all right?' Black Tip asked her.

'I'm okay – just a few nips.'

'A lot more than I have.' He looked at Nightshade and was glad to see she hadn't been injured.

A few minutes later, Whiskers rejoined them and they were relieved to find that the mink weren't giving chase.

Seeing that the otter was bleeding profusely, Black Tip said, 'You've been bitten quite a lot.'

'Don't worry about me,' Whiskers replied. 'My skin's a lot tougher than yours.' He lay down and began to lick his wounds. 'But we were lucky to escape. If they had attacked us in greater numbers we were done for.'

'If it hadn't been for you and Black Tip, I'd have been done for,' said Bluebell. 'You too Nightshade. You were very brave.'

'They didn't attack me at all,' said Nightshade, who was

cleaning the blood from the fur of her friend. 'I wonder why?'

Whiskers looked up and smiled. 'You must have a charmed life. When you left they decided to go for me instead, and I'm glad.'

'Why?' asked Nightshade.

'Because, unlike you I can fight them in the water just as easily as on the land, if not better. Furthermore, I'm bigger than they are and I can hold my breath under water a lot longer than they can.'

'So much for trying to talk to them,' said Black Tip.

Bluebell got up and went over to see how Whiskers was. 'They're very vicious,' she observed, seeing how badly he had been bitten.

'It's in their nature to be vicious,' he told her, 'and hunger makes them worse.'

When they reported back to Old Sage Brush, the old fox nodded. 'Ratwiddle said we don't have to climb trees to catch fish. Maybe he was trying to tell us there's an easier way.'

'That's what Nightshade thinks he meant,' said Black Tip.

Vickey went over and lay down beside Whiskers. Seeing that his wounds were still bleeding, she said, 'I didn't think the mink would have attacked an otter.'

Whiskers smiled. 'We may be related, but somehow I don't think this blood is the same as theirs.'

When Old Sage Brush came over to talk to Whiskers,

Vickey returned to look after Black Tip.

'I wonder why the mink didn't attack Nightshade?' she said.

'I don't know,' Black Tip replied. 'Whiskers thinks she must have a charmed life.'

'You mean, like Ratwiddle?'

'Something like that I suppose. But there's only one Ratwiddle.'

Vickey nodded. Nightshade had heard Ratwiddle when the rest of them couldn't. Now she seemed to know what he meant when he said they didn't have to climb trees to catch fish. And the mink seemed to be afraid of her. Strange...

'Tell me Whiskers,' said Old Sage Brush, 'do mink eat squirrels?'

'Do you mean red squirrels or grey squirrels?'

Old Sage Brush smiled. 'As I have told my friends who escaped from the farm, colour is only fur deep. But in this instance, I refer to the greys as they are greater in number.'

'I gather they don't particularly like the taste of squirrel.'

Old Sage Brush nodded. 'If they did, could they catch them?'

'The reds are not so easy to catch as they feed up in the trees. But they could catch the greys as they feed on the ground.'

'Ah, so that's what Ratwiddle meant! The answer to our problem is not to be found in the trees or in the water, but on the ground.' The old fox called to the others. 'Now, all of you gather round. Here's what I think we should do.'

Once again Whiskers led Black Tip, Bluebell and Night-shade into the forest. Stopping at the clearing where they had seen the tree cat catching the grey squirrel, they hid in the shrubbery and waited. They reckoned that as the tree cat had already eaten one of the squirrels, it wouldn't return for some time. The squirrels probably thought the same, and it wasn't long before they returned to the ground to search for buried nuts and other seeds. However, they were unaware that another hunter was waiting for them.

Having taking up different positions in the shrubbery, the three foxes left the squirrels with nowhere to run and suc-ceeded in catching two of them. Whiskers then dissected one of the squirrels and left the pieces along the lake shore. At the same time, the foxes dissected the other one and left a trail of meat between the shore and the clearing. It wasn't long before the hungry mink discovered the pieces of meat on the shore, and when they had devoured those they looked around for more. They soon found the pieces the foxes had left for them and followed the trail into the wood.

By the time the mink reached the clearing they had got a good taste of squirrel, and while they didn't normally like it, their hunger made them crave for more. The foxes and the otter were gone now, but the only scent the mink were interested in was squirrel, and they could smell the scent of many squirrels around the base of the tree. They looked up, wondering where the squirrels had gone. They also wondered when they would be back, and realised that they had discovered a new hunting ground…

'So what do we do now?' asked Bluebell when they returned to the earth.

Old Sage Brush smiled. 'We don't do anything. If I'm not mistaken, the grey squirrels will now be hunted by the white mink as well as the tree cat. They'll be forced to move and when they do, the mink will follow. So will the tree cat. The red squirrels will be left alone and the balance of nature will be restored.'

'But there are only two red squirrels left,' said Nightshade.

'True,' Old Sage Brush told her. 'But their breeding time is near and, hopefully, they will soon be able to breed in peace.'

'Eat in peace too,' added Nightshade.

'We have to eat,' said Black Tip, 'and the ducks have gone.'

'Ducks come and go,' replied the old fox. 'When they find the mink have gone, they'll be back.'

'What about the fish?' asked Whiskers. 'The mink have taken them all.'

'Oh I doubt if they've taken them all,' said the old fox. 'It's a big lake. I imagine there are still some left and, given time there'll be more.'

The otter blew through his nose as if to dislodge something from his whiskers. 'If there are any fish left, I couldn't find them. Which reminds me. I was on my way to another lake.'

Vickey smiled. 'As Ratwiddle said, you don't have to climb trees to catch fish!'

'Now Vickey,' Whiskers responded, 'what would a fox know about catching fish?' There was, she could see, a twinkle in his eye and in deference to the old fox he added, 'Anyway, I'll try the lake one more time. Then I'm off.'

'And I'm off to hunt,' said Black Tip. 'I don't know about the rest of you, but I'm hungry.'

'I don't fancy a squirrel myself,' Vickey called after him, 'but I wouldn't mind a rabbit!'

ELEVEN

THE HONEY TRAP

Before leaving, Whiskers cautioned Old Sage Brush and his friends to stay clear of the Forest of Fear until the white mink had gone, and even avoid the fields beyond.

'When the mink have driven the grey squirrels from the forest,' he told them, 'they will attack everything in their path – the ducks in the farmyard, the chickens in the coops, even the lambs in the fields. Then the shooters will destroy them – foxes too if they come upon them.'

'Lambs?' said Old Sage Brush. 'And we might get the blame.'

With those few words, Whiskers went his way in search of another lake and they went theirs in search of the Hills of the Long Low Cloud.

Vickey, who always worried about the welfare of the

weaker members of their group, was relieved that Hop-along had decided to return to the Land of Sinna, but now she worried about Old Sage Brush.

'Do you think perhaps he has taken on too much?' she asked her mate.

'He's a tough old dog,' Black Tip assured her.

'Still, I can't help noticing how frail he is.'

Black Tip nodded. 'I know. But he's the only one who can decide when he's had enough.'

Vickey lowered her voice. 'Sometimes I wonder if the Hills of the Long Low Cloud really exist. I mean, I never heard of them before. And none of the foxes who came to see us at Beech Paw had ever seen them.'

'There are some who say the Great White Fox doesn't exist, just because they've never seen him, but I believe he does.'

'Me too,' said Vickey. 'But still... I wonder.'

'Why would Old Sage Brush take us on such a journey if the hills don't exist?' asked Black tip. 'And it has turned out to be such a dangerous one.'

'All our journeys had their dangers,' Vickey recalled, 'But I suppose on this one we're not fully in control of what we do – or should I say, what they do.'

Black Tip glanced over at Bluebell and Nightshade who were dozing nearby.

'But I think they're doing very well,' Vickey hastened to add. 'They've learned a lot since we started out and they've shown themselves to be very brave.'

Black Tip nodded. 'By the time we reach the hills they should be able to survive on their own.'

Vickey was about to say, 'If we ever reach them,' but decided against it and said nothing. She was now more concerned about Old Sage Brush and whether he would survive.

After a while Bluebell and Nightshade came over and lay down beside them. Bluebell's fur was clear of blood now, but the mink had left their mark and underneath the fur she was very sore. 'Tell us more about the other journeys you made with Old Sage Brush,' she said.

Vickey threw a knowing glance at Black Tip, wondering for a moment if Bluebell had heard them talking, but decided it was just a coincidence.

'Well,' she said, 'as we told you before, we went on our first journey with him because, like you, we had much to learn.'

'And you said you went to Man's Place,' said Nightshade. 'Tell us again. What was it like?'

Vickey sniffed, 'Smelly. Man had left his rubbish in bags and his dogs were rooting in it for food.'

'Were you not afraid of them?'

'Of course,' Black Tip admitted. 'But as I said, we met a fox called Scavenger who showed us the way and the dogs were so busy rooting in the rubbish they didn't see us.'

'Were you not more afraid of the giant ginger cats?' asked Bluebell.

Vickey nodded. 'It would be a brave fox who wouldn't be afraid of them. They were much bigger than anything you could imagine, but we only saw them through the wire.'

'Are you saying they were in wire cages like the ones we were in?' asked Nightshade.

'No, but there were very high fences and walls to keep them in.'

'And who fed them?'

'Man did,' said Black Tip.

Bluebell shivered. 'Oh, I don't like the sound of that.'

'Man seemed to be very good to them,' said Vickey. 'He gave them huge chunks of meat to eat.'

'Still,' said Bluebell, 'I don't like the sound of it.'

'As far as we could see,' Black Tip told her, 'they weren't there to be killed for their fur. Man came in great numbers to see them – them and other kinds of animals as well.'

'Do these kinds of animals live in this world of yours?' asked Nightshade.

Black Tip laughed. 'Of course not. The only cats you're going to come across are smaller than we are. So there's no need to be afraid.'

Vickey decided it was time to change the subject, and seeing that Nightshade was licking her lips, said, 'You'll also come across things you haven't yet tasted – things that will give you much pleasure.'

'Like what?' asked Bluebell.

'Well, honey for instance. It's made by the bees and is very sweet.'

Bluebell smiled. 'It sounds lovely. Where do the bees make it?'

'In honeycombs – up in the trees. But the bees guard it with their lives and if they sting you it can be every bit as sore as the bite of a mink.'

'Where can we see one of these honeycombs?' asked Nightshade.

'I don't remember seeing them in winter,' Black Tip told her, 'but man sometimes gets the bees to make honey for him.'

'He builds places for them to live in,' Vickey explained. 'They are white, just like Snowflake. If we come across one, we'll show you.'

'I can see we still have a lot of learn,' said Bluebell.

Vickey smiled. 'We have learned a lot from Old Sage Brush and we still have a lot to learn.'

As they continued their journey, the Forest of Fear and the creatures that inhabited it, became but a memory and were well left behind. Frost settled on the fields at night and the clear air revealed a sky that seemed to sparkle more brightly than ever. The wide eye of gloomglow smiled upon those seeking the Land of the Long Low Cloud, and the Great Running Fox was their guiding star.

Bluebell and Nightshade were good learners. They now

knew how to mark the position where the Great Running Fox touched down before taking off again on its own journey across the sky. They had learned how to hunt rabbits by day and rats by night, and a few days later they learned something else.

Vickey was out hunting with Nightshade, when they came upon a small house standing on its own on the outskirts of a village. On the road outside was a wheelie bin awaiting collection.

Vickey walked around the bin, stopped and looked up. It seemed very high, not like the ones man used to use to put his rubbish in when she was younger. They were about half the size of this one and it was easy to dislodge their covers.

'It's smelly,' Nightshade whispered.

'It's full of man's waste,' Vickey told her. 'But there's a lot of food in there too – a kind of food you've never tasted before.'

As the two of them looked up at the wheelie bin again, Nightshade wondered how they were going to get at the food.

Vickey jumped up on to the low garden wall and from there on to the bin. Cautiously she put her front paws on one of the handles, leaned forward and tried to rock it. Nothing happened and she whispered to Nightshade to join her.

'Do what I'm doing,' she told her.

Nightshade put her forepaws on the adjoining handle and together they began to rock the bin.

'Lean forward,' Vickey said, 'and put your full weight on it.'

They began to rock the bin again and seconds later it toppled over. They jumped clear as the lid flew open and some of the contents spilled out on to the street. In the nearby house a dog barked and they took a few steps away from the bin, ready to run.

It was a small dog, Vickey reckoned, and it sounded as if it was inside the house, not out in the yard. 'It's okay, it's inside,' she assured Nightshade. 'Now, eat what you can and what you can't eat take with you.'

Nightshade didn't like the smell of the rubbish, but as she picked her way through it she found pieces of gristle that man had found too tough to eat, chicken bones that had been picked clean and some spare ribs on which there was still some meat. She also came across a small container and was licking a sweet liquid that clung to the inside of it when the bin tumbled off the footpath and onto the street. The dog began to bark again, and there was the sound of a door opening. At the same time two over-fed cats approached them.

'Come on,' said Vickey. 'Let's go!' She grabbed a mouthful of spare ribs, Nightshade grabbed some chicken bones, and they sped through the nearest hedge.

'Damned foxes!' they heard someone shout, but the dog didn't give chase and a short time later they stopped in a field to get their breath.

'Pity we had to leave the rest of the food behind,'

panted Nightshade.

'We're lucky we got as much as we did. Anyway, the gok-goks are gathering. There'll be none of it left by the time they've finished.'

Man, they could hear, was putting the bin back on its wheels and gathering up the rubbish. He was still cursing the foxes as he returned to the house, leaving the gulls to swoop and squabble over the scraps of food that were left on the ground.

'Come on,' said Vickey, 'let's take these bones back. We can share them with the others.

Nightshade was tempted to lie down and have the chicken bones all to herself. Instead, she ran her tongue around her mouth again to savour the taste of the Chinese takeaway. Then she picked up the bones and followed Vickey.

As the others shared the spoils of their raid on the wheelie bin, Bluebell asked Nightshade, 'Was it honey you got? You said it was sweet.'

'I don't know – but I wouldn't mind some more of it.'

'I don't think it was honey,' said Vickey. 'Anyway, you can't go back there.'

'Could you show us where to get some honey?' asked Bluebell.

Vickey shrugged. 'I don't know. Places where bees make honey aren't easy to find.'

'And remember what Old Sage Brush told the cubs?' said

Black Tip. 'He said – what was it now, Vickey? – he said, you can't lick honey from a briar.'

'What a strange thing to say,' said Bluebell. 'What did he mean by that?'

'I think,' Vickey told her, 'it was his way of warning them that they couldn't get honey without disturbing the bees. But, of course, they paid no heed.'

'And did they get any honey?' asked Nightshade.

Black Tip shook his head. 'No, but our cub got stung. Her mouth was very swollen and it was some time before she could eat any solid food.'

'Still,' Vickey added, 'we all have to learn, and I suppose there's no harm in looking. Black Tip, you stay here with Old Sage Brush. I'll take the two of them out and see what we can find.'

When, a short time later, they stopped to look at a mass of hoof prints, the two farmed foxes assumed they had been made by sheep.

'They look like the hoof prints of sheep,' Vickey told them. 'But they're different. And so is the scent.'

Nightshade sniffed the air. 'So what are they?'

'They're goats.'

'Are they like sheep?' asked Bluebell.

'No, they're bigger, and if they butt you with their horns you'll know all about it.'

Curious to see what goats looked like, Bluebell and Nightshade followed Vickey up a hill, the lower slopes of which were covered in shrubbery. The goats, she pointed out, had been nibbling at the shrubs, some of which were prickly and the two of them reckoned that these animals must have very strong mouths.

'There they are,' Vickey whispered.

Looking up the hill, Bluebell and Nightshade saw a herd of goats hopping around the rocky summit.

'That one standing on top, he's their leader,' Vickey told them.

The billy goat, they could see, had positioned himself on the highest rock. He had long curved horns and a beard, and he appeared to be looking out for danger. But if he was, he didn't move as they approached. The other goats hopped around a bit on the lower rocks but he showed no signs of fear.

'I see what you mean about the horns!' said Nightshade. 'I wouldn't like to be butted by him.'

Leaving the goats to their rocky outcrop, they made their way around the hill and into a small valley beyond.

'Remember I told you man keeps bees to make honey?' said Vickey. 'Well, you see those white things down there, that's where he keeps them.'

The foxes were now on a farm where the owner made cheese from the goats' milk, grew organic vegetables and had many beehives. He had placed his hives on the south-facing slope of the valley to give the bees a flight path across fields of white clover and wild flowers from which they could produce high quality honey. In the autumn he had removed much of the honey, leaving the remainder as food for the bees in winter. When it snowed he decided they might need some extra food and provided this in the form of a soft home-made candy consisting mostly of sugar. As far as he was concerned, it was a fair trade. He got the honey and the bees got the candy.

The bees, of course, didn't know the difference. Nor did the foxes who listened at one of the hives. They could hear the sound of the bees as the outer ones moved in and the inner ones move out in a continual movement to keep warm. Their keen sense of smell also detected a very pleasant aroma coming from inside.

'Come on Nightshade,' said Vickey. 'Let's see if we can topple it, the way we toppled the bin.'

Jumping on to the flat roof of the hive the two of them put their paws on the front edge and tried to rock it, but it didn't move. Being made of wood, it was much heavier than the wheelie bin, which was made of plastic. It was also lower and sat firmly on four short legs on a level base. Vickey asked Bluebell to help, but it refused to budge.

Reluctantly they gave up and retreated to the other side of the valley which was covered with gorse.

'I didn't even see a bee,' Bluebell complained.

'Maybe it's just as well,' Vickey told her. 'They can't penetrate our fur, but a sting on the lips or the nose can be very painful.'

Hearing the bleating of the goats, Vickey looked up. Above them, members of the herd hopped from one rock to another, while the billy goat still watched impassively from the highest rock.

'Goats love hopping on to things,' she murmured, more to herself than the others. 'I wonder if we got them down among the hives, would they hop on to them.'

'And knock them over,' said Nightshade. 'It might work. They're much bigger than us.'

'But how are we going to get them to go to the hives?' asked Bluebell. 'They didn't seem to be afraid of us.'

'They can be very stubborn all right,' said Vickey. 'Let's go up and see.'

When they had circled around until they were behind the goats, Vickey said, 'You two stay here. Make sure they don't run back this way. I'll see if I can move them on.'

In spite of Vickey's arrival, the goats stayed where they were. Bluebell went up to help her, and the two of them ran in among the herd to try and scare them. A few of the goats moved around a bit, glanced back at the foxes and bleated, but didn't look as if they were going anywhere. It was only when Nightshade joined in that the herd became agitated. The billy goat then hopped down off his perch and led the others into the valley.

'They seemed to be afraid of you, Nightshade,' said Vickey.

Nightshade smiled. 'Maybe they haven't seen a black fox before!'

The goats did indeed seem to be afraid of Nightshade and they managed to usher the herd across to the other side of the valley. There the billy goat stopped and, taking their lead from him, the others stopped too and idly chewed their cuds. After a bit more coaxing, the foxes got them to wander in among the beehives. It was slow going, but Vickey told Bluebell and Nightshade to be patient. Then, to their delight, several of the goats hopped up on to the hives. However, the hives didn't move.

'What are we going to do now?' asked Bluebell.

'Maybe they've shifted the hives a bit,' said Vickey. 'Let's see if we can topple them now.'

On their approach the goats moved across the slope a little bit, stopping to watch as the foxes hopped up on to some of the hives they had just vacated.

'It's no good,' Vickey said at last. 'They won't move.'

Just then they heard the sound of a horn. Bluebell and Nightshade didn't know what it was, but Vickey did. It was the sound of a hunting horn!

'Let's get out of here!' she exclaimed. 'Hurry.'

Vickey set off across the valley with all the speed she could muster, but when she paused and looked around was horrified to see that the other two hadn't followed her.

Bluebell and Nightshade were still standing on the hives, wondering why Vickey had run off, when another fox streaked down the slope towards them.

'Run!' he cried. 'Run for your lives!'

The two had seen no bees and saw no reason to run, but as the other fox streaked away among the hives, he shouted, 'It's the howling dogs!'

Because they were lower than the fields adjoining the valley, it was only now that Bluebell and Nightshade could hear the cry of the hounds. As they hopped off the hives and ran, the howling suddenly got louder and they knew the hounds were close behind.

Vickey was in a panic. The hounds were bounding down the slope now. The other fox had disappeared but Bluebell and Nightshade had delayed too long. Without the head start she had got, the hounds were sure to catch them.

However, the hounds had come down the slope too fast. Unable to stop, some had no option but to jump on to the hives. Their weight and speed toppled them and the different sections came apart, spilling the bees, honeycombs, candy and all, on to the grass. The hounds that followed tripped on the broken hives and fell. Their lolling tongues discovered a sweetness they had not experienced before and they began to lick it. As they did so, they found themselves in a cloud of bees. Angered by being so rudely awakened from their winter slumber the bees immediately descended on them, stinging them on the lips, noses and eyes.

Meanwhile, the hounds that had toppled the hives ran into the goats, some of which lowered their heads and butted them. They retreated, only to be attacked by the bees as well. To add to the confusion, the riders now came galloping over the hill and in spite of strenuous efforts to rein in their mounts, came crashing down the slope too. Some of the riders were unseated. They ended up among the hives and the bees attacked them. The horses were also being stung and the members of the hunt who were still in the saddle were trying to stay there.

By this time, Bluebell and Nightshade had joined Vickey on the other side of the valley, and the three of them watched in amazement as huntsmen and hounds milled around among the hives. The hounds were yelping and the men were shouting. One man was cracking a whip, while another was making urgent calls on his hunting horn. But for all their efforts, it seemed a long time before they were able to extricate themselves from the chaos they had caused. As they beat a hasty retreat, the horses were bucking, the hounds were turning their heads and snapping and it was obvious they were still being attacked by the bees.

Bluebell was trembling. 'When you told us to run, we didn't know why.'

'I'm sorry,' said Vickey, 'but there was just no time to

explain.'

Nightshade turned to go. 'We'd better get back.'

Vickey smiled. 'And leave that honey behind? I don't think so.'

The bees, they found, were still angrily defending the broken honeycombs, but they managed to get a lick of honey before being driven off. So sweet was the taste – so sublimely sweet to a palate that was accustomed to meat – that they decided to go back for more. This time they managed to snatch some candy. Their mouths were still watering from the honey, and by the time they stopped running the candy had melted on their tongues to give them another exquisite taste of sweetness.

As they licked their lips, they realised there was no way they could take any of it back to Old Sage Brush and Black Tip. Nevertheless, they took back a great story – and a few stings to prove it. They didn't say they had deliberately drawn the hounds on to the beehives, because they hadn't. At the same time they didn't try to dispel the idea.

'I wonder where the other fox went?' wondered Old Sage Brush.

Vickey shook her head. 'I've no idea. He was running fast and I wouldn't be surprised if he's still running.'

TWELVE

A NARROW SQUEAK

Some distance beyond the village where Vickey and Nightshade had toppled the wheelie bin, stood a big house surrounded by hundreds of acres of land that included a farm and mature woods of oak and beech. A belt of oak trees also encircled the entire the estate as if to protect those who lived in the house from public view. However, times had changed. The young people who had grown up there had gone their separate ways. Their ageing parents could no longer operate the farm and, finding the house too big for just the two of them, had put the estate up for sale.

The 'For Sale' signs had attracted few, apart from one or two locals who took the opportunity to go in with dog and gun and hunt for pheasant. Then the news had come that the estate had been bought by a group of wealthy business people. Soon afterwards, a high fence was erected along the entire length of the boundary wall and signs of a different kind were posted on it. They warned people to 'Keep Out' – and for good reason, as the estate was now being used for quite a different purpose.

As far as the foxes were concerned all land, whether public or private, was theirs. They had failed to find an earth for the night and when Black Tip came across the scent of another fox he followed it until he came to a small drain in the base of the boundary wall. A dribble of water was coming from it, but as the other fox had gone into it he had no hesitation in doing the same. It was quite a long drain, and when they emerged they found themselves in a patch of shrubbery.

It was almost daylight now and when they heard the harsh cry of a cock pheasant breaking into flight, Old Sage Brush nodded with satisfaction as pheasant was his favourite food. Then, farther in, he got a strong smell of what he thought was cat. The others got it too, but assured him there was no sign of a cat. There were red squirrels in the trees, but no grey squirrels, or even a tree cat. More importantly, there was no sign of man. As they had travelled most of the night, Black Tip suggested that they rest first and hunt later. But as the others nestled down in a patch of rhododendron bushes, Bluebell and Nightshade couldn't resist the temptation to go out and explore.

Having been caged for most of their lives, the two of them

felt a sense of exhilaration when they surveyed the country-side – woods to one side, a farm on the other, but no hedges or wire fences as far as they could see. To them, a place without wire was a wonderful place, a place where they were free to do as they pleased. Had they looked at what lay behind them they would have been less pleased, but it was what lay before them that attracted their attention.

As they wandered around looking for something to do, they spotted the fox that had led the howling dogs on to the beehives. He was standing beside what looked like a decaying log licking his lips. They could also see what they thought were bees buzzing around the log which lay on the grass at the foot of a slight rise. Thinking that the other fox had found a comb of wild honey like the ones Vickey had told them about, thoughts of the sugary sweetness watered their tongues, and they galloped over to it in the hope of getting more.

Bluebell and Nightshade had never felt the heat of the sun in their cages and didn't know the difference between winter when bees stayed in the warmth of their hives and summer when they foraged for nectar to make honey. Nor at that distance could they tell the difference between a bee and a fly. On their approach the other fox ran off, and they found it was not bees that had attracted their attention but several large flies. They also found that the flies were not buzzing around a honeycomb in a rotten log, but the carcass of an animal to which clung tatters of skin and a few morsels of meat.

The two foxes were disappointed that they were not to enjoy the sweetness of the bees once more, but were delighted to have found food of another kind and leapt upon the bones to snatch the meat from the flies. Inexperienced as they were, they had not stopped to question the presence of such a carcass.

Although they weren't aware of it, Vickey had been following the two of them, and her amusement at their antics turned to concern when she saw the size of the carcass. She immediately asked herself the questions the other two should have asked. Where had such a carcass come from and what had stripped it of its flesh? She might also have wondered about the presence of flies in winter but for the fact that something much larger attracted her attention.

When squeezing under the boundary wall, Black Tip and Vickey had failed to notice that above it was a fence as high as the one they had seen in the Land of the Giant Ginger Cats. And had they looked back they would have seen another one among the trees, a short distance from where they had emerged from the drain. The fences had been erected by the new owners, for they were in the process of turning the estate into a wildlife park. Most families, they reasoned, couldn't afford to go to Africa, but could afford to tour the park and see some of its exotic creatures, including lions, living almost as freely as they did on the African plains.

Looking around, Vickey was horrified to see what she called a giant ginger cat lying on the top of the rise. It shook its huge head to dislodge a few more flies that had the temerity to torment it, and in doing so flicked out its thick mane. However, it was the movement of the tail that told her what it intended to do to those who dared take the meat that had been left for it. Its tail was slowly switching back and forth in the way she had seen a tom cat do before it pounced, and she knew the giant ginger cat was about to pounce on Bluebell and Nightshade.

'Run!' she cried. 'Run!' At the same time Vickey realised that she couldn't lead the two of them back to the drain where they had come in. It was too far away and in any case, she would risk drawing the giant cat on to Black Tip and Old Sage Brush. So she took off in the opposite direction. As she did so, the lion sprang into action.

Seeing it bounding down the slope towards them, Bluebell and Nightshade fled. They had no idea where they were going, but in a blind panic to get away, followed Vickey as fast as their legs could carry them. How the huge cat had come to be there they couldn't imagine, but it seemed to have leapt right out of the story Vickey had told them. In that story, she and her friends had hunted in a place where the cats were in big wire pens, but this cat was free to hunt and was hunting them.

Black Tip, meanwhile, had stayed in the rhododendron bushes with Old Sage Brush. The old fox was tired and as always Black Tip was watching over him. 'Let me be your eyes,' he had once told him and while the old fox might lead the way when it came to cunning, it was Black Tip who led him on their journeys from the Land of Sinna.

From the cover of the bushes, Black Tip had watched his mate as she followed Bluebell and Nighshade, and his eyes opened wide in disbelief when he saw them racing toward the woods followed by a giant ginger cat. He immediately woke Old Sage Brush and told him what had happened. It took the old fox a few moments to realise he wasn't dreaming, but when the import of what Black Tip was saying sank in, he agreed that the best thing to do was stay put.

Old Sage Brush, of course, had not been able to see any of the animals in what they called the Land of the Giant Ginger Cats, but the roars he had heard coming from the zoo had been very frightening. He thought the others had been more than a little foolhardy to venture into it and very lucky to get back out. Now it seemed they had wandered into the domain of the giant ginger cats again, and this time he was right in there with them. Nevertheless, as Black Tip told him what was happening, it was not his own life, but the lives of Vickey and the two other foxes that he feared for.

As Bluebell and Nightshade ran through the woods after Vickey, they caught a glimpse of a very tall animal with a long high neck running awkwardly away to their right. A short distance farther on, a herd of ponies with black and white stripes scattered in confusion, some kicking up their hind legs as if to ward off the giant cat. If that was their fear, they needn't have worried. The cat was in its own fenced-off domain – and so were they. Furthermore, it had eyes only for the foxes that had dared take its food, and it was now closing in on them.

Whatever about Vickey who was a short distance ahead of them, Bluebell and Nightshade could hear the great padded feet of their pursuer pounding after them. They could almost feel its breath upon their backs and feared its great jaws were about to snap them up when, to their surprise, another fox cut across their path. It was the one they had seen standing beside what they thought was a log licking its lips.

'Split up,' he panted. 'Don't run together. Scatter.'

Suddenly the great cat saw, not three but four foxes running away in different directions. Not knowing which to chase, it turned to go after the one that had cut across its path. Then it changed its mind and resumed its chase of the others, only to discover that they had all disappeared into the shrubbery. Frustrated, it lay down, growled loudly and thrashed its tail impatiently.

Having laid low for what seemed a long time, Vickey eventually found the courage to move and succeeded in locating Bluebell and Nightshade who were hiding in a clump of bushes. They were trembling with fright, and Bluebell whimpered, 'I think we were safer back in our cage.'

'Safer?' said Vickey. 'I doubt it. Here at least you can run for your lives. Back in your cage you couldn't.'

Neither Bluebell nor Nightshade were reassured by this for they could hear the giant cat growling and roaring not far away and they got quite a fright when the other fox suddenly appeared beside them.

'You walk with much stealth,' Vickey told him.

'In this land you must,' replied the other fox. 'Otherwise you would end up as food for the giant cats.'

'You mean there are more?' asked Vickey.

The other fox nodded. 'There's also a female and several large cubs. The one who chased you is their leader.'

'Thank you for distracting it,' said Bluebell. 'I shudder to think what would have happened if you hadn't.'

The other fox smiled. 'The cat is big and runs only in spurts. I can run faster and for longer.'

Vickey, who had been watching him intently, said, 'But surely we have met before. You're the fox that outran the howling dogs at the beehives. And if I'm not mistaken it wasn't the first time you outran them – you're Running Fox!'

'That's right. And you're Vickey. How could I forget?'

'So it was your scent we followed?'

'It was – if you came in under the wall. But tell me, who are your friends? I have never seen such colours in a fox.'

Vickey introduced him to Bluebell and Nightshade and told him how they had escaped from the cages in the fur farm.

'When we saw the flies we thought they were bees,' explained Bluebell.

'And that they were buzzing around a honeycomb,' said Nightshade.

Running Fox smiled. 'You don't see bees at this time of year.'

'Flies either,' said Vickey. 'So where did they come from?'

'They live in the place man has made for the cats. It's quite warm – and dirty, so they can survive there even when it's cold outside.'

'But they were outside.'

'Some of them stay in the long hair of the leader of the cats. It keeps them warm I suppose. And when the cat goes out to eat the food man has left for it, they brave the cold for a short time to buzz around it.'

'And we thought they were bees,' said Nightshade. 'You're right, Vickey, we do have a lot to learn.'

'As I told you before,' Vickey replied, 'we all do, and for a start we have to figure out how to get away from this cat.'

As they talked, the growling of the giant ginger cat rose to a roar and fell to a ravenous rumble in its great throat.

'I think we should make a run for it,' said Bluebell in a tremulous voice. 'I mean, the cat's sure to find us if we just lie here.'

'It won't move until it's rested,' Running Fox assured her. 'So we must rest too before we move on.'

'Move on where?' asked Nightshade. 'If there are more cats, we may run into them.'

'I know this land well,' Running Fox told her. 'And I know the cats. At night time they stay in the place man has made for them, and during the day they lie up on a small hill not far away. One of the big ones stays with the cubs while the other goes out to look for food. But they don't hunt. Man leaves out food for them.'

'But this one is hunting us,' said Bluebell.

Running Fox shook his head. 'No it isn't. Well, not for food. I think it gets bored lying around. It's probably just chasing us to amuse itself. It's chased me before.'

'You mean it's just chasing us for fun?' asked Vickey.

'Something like that.'

Nightshade shivered. 'It may be fun for the cat, but it's not much fun for us. If it catches us it'll kill us.'

'Maybe we could get out the way we came in,' Vickey suggested.

Running Fox shook his head. 'We'd never make it. It's too far away. But there's an earth not far from here. I use it quite often. We could make a run for that. What do you think?'

'I'm ready,' Vickey replied, 'but we have two friends out there somewhere and one of them is too old to run – Old Sage Brush. You met him before. You helped Skulking Dog save his daughter Sinnéad in the Land of the Howling Dogs, remember?'

Running Fox nodded. 'Yes, I remember. But where is he?'

'Black Tip is with him – out there among the bushes.'

'Well, they should be all right – so long as they sit tight. It's us the big cat is after.'

Bluebell cocked an ear. 'It's stopped growling. Maybe it's gone back to the others.'

Running Fox shook its head. 'No, that means it's on the move again. It's looking for us. Time to go. Follow me and if it gets too close split up, the way you did the last time.'

When Running Fox gave the signal, he raced off through the trees and the others followed The big cat roared and seconds later came pounding after them. Once again Bluebell and Nightshade couldn't tell which was louder, the pounding of the pads of the cat or the pounding of their hearts. Running Fox was travelling at great speed, a speed even Vickey could barely match, but the fear of being caught by the giant beast drove all of them on.

With every bound, the big cat drew closer. Vickey could see that Running Fox wasn't deviating from his path and the other two could see that Vickey wasn't deviating from hers. If they split up they would never find the earth, so they kept going. The big cat was almost on them now and one of them, they feared, would surely die. The cat was about to leap and they were about to split up, when to their enormous relief they saw Running Fox disappear down the open hole of an earth. With a last desperate effort, they flung themselves in after him. Bluebell was last in and as the cat landed with a loud thud, it made a swipe at her with its great paw, missing her tail by a hair's breadth.

In the darkness of the earth they lay down and fought to get their breaths back, while outside the great cat lay down, yawned and licked its lips. The thought of their narrow escape made them tremble and the presence of the cat at the entrance to the earth made them tremble even more. Anxiously they waited for the cat to go, but it stayed where it was, occasionally putting in a paw to see if it could catch one of them in its claws.

'What are we going to do?' Bluebell asked of no one in particular.

'We're just going to have to wait,' Running Fox told her.

'Wait for what?' asked Nightshade. 'There's no sign of it going.'

'When man brings it food it may go. It depends on whether it's hungry, or whether it wants to play games.'

'Can it dig us out?' asked Bluebell.

'It's not the digging type. We're safe down here.'

'Which is more than can be said for Old Sage Brush and Black Tip,' added Vickey.

As they pondered on their predicament, Vickey said,

'Maybe there's another way out.'

Running Fox shook his head. 'This is not a badger sett. There's only one way in – and the same way out.'

Vickey lowered her nose on to her forepaws in despair. The four of them, she realised, were prisoners of the cat because they couldn't get out, while Old Sage Brush and Black Tip were in even greater danger because they couldn't get in.

While all this was going on, the keeper whose job it was to feed the lions, was involved in a trial of strength with an even bigger creature in the farmyard. He was unaware that the male lion was hunting other animals in its area of the park. Nor did he know that the lioness was now taking the cubs to join her mate in the hope of giving them a fox to play with and tease in their own cruel game of cat and mouse

From his hiding place in the rhododendron bushes where he was minding Old Sage Brush, Black Tip was dismayed to see Vickey and the others being pursued by the giant ginger cat. He lost sight of them when they went into the woods, and his relief knew no bounds when he saw them emerge and reach the safety of the earth. His fears for them grew again when he saw more cats gathering outside the earth, but there was nothing he could do to help them. His immediate concern was for Old Sage Brush, and he realised that while the cats were besetting the others, it was an opportunity for him to get the old fox to safety. He also knew they would never make it across the open ground to the place where they came in. The old fox was too slow and the cats were too fast.

'There are some farm buildings near the big house,' Black Tip told him. 'If we circle around away from the cats we might be able to get to them. But, if the cats see us...'

'I know,' said Old Sage Brush, 'but it matters not if they catch me. I have lived a long life – longer than most foxes. You, however, might make it and in doing so draw them away from Vickey and the others.'

It was typical of the old fox, Black Tip thought. His own life was in danger, yet his concern was for his friends.

'I don't think they're in any immediate danger,' Black Tip added, 'unless the big cats try and dig them out. But we are in great danger out here in the open and I know Vickey would want us to move.'

'If we tread softly,' said the old fox, 'we might make it.

Black Tip smiled. No fox, he knew, could tread more softly than Old Sage Brush. Blind he might be, but he had never been known to put a paw wrong. How else could he have lived so long?

Without further ado, Black Tip led him out of the side of the bushes away from where the giant ginger cats were sitting around the earth. Not a twig cracked or a leaf rustled as they made their way among the trees, through the shrubbery and the long grass and over to where the farm buildings were encircled by another high wall. Looking back they saw that the cats hadn't moved, but from inside the walls they heard the roar of another animal. It was a big animal, judging by the sound, and it seemed to be highly agitated.

'I've heard that sound before,' whispered Old Sage Brush.

'And I've seen the animal that makes it,' said Black Tip. 'It was in Man's Place.'

'What was it like?'

'It was the one with the nose so long it almost touched the ground. It had huge flapping ears, two long teeth and feet like the stumps of trees.'

'It sounds very big.'

'It was very big. In fact, it was the biggest animal we saw in Man's Place.'

The roaring had got louder and more frenzied now and they sank into the long grass in case the giant ginger cats might look back and see them.

Black Tip said nothing, but as he surveyed the wall he could see they were in a worse predicament now than when they were in the rhododendron bushes. He had hoped to get sanctuary for the old fox in among the farm buildings, but the only access was by a huge pair of wooden doors. Both were closed and there wasn't even a small space at the bottom where they could squeeze in. They were trapped.

Suddenly there was another roar from the farmyard, the huge wooden doors burst open and out charged the animal

175

with the long nose and big ears. Its nose was now curled up over its head, foamy water was dribbling from its mouth, its two long white teeth were gleaming, and it was trumpeting in a way that showed it was greatly distressed. At least, that's what Black Tip thought as he relayed what he was seeing to Old Sage Brush.

'What's it doing now?' asked the old fox as a different sounds came to his ears.

'It's gone into the trees. It's ... It's just crashing through them...'

The elephant was the most recent acquisition for the wildlife park. It had been bought from a circus that had run into financial trouble, and its keeper, who had also acted as the circus strong strongman, was recruited to look after it. At first the elephant had been very easy to manage. It did what it was told and was a great favourite with visitors. However, when out on its own it would reach up with its trunk and pull branches off the trees so that it could feed on them, even put its head to some of the smaller trees and push them to the ground. To prevent such damage to the woods, it had been decided to keep it indoors and only take it out occasionally for a walk or so that visitors could see it as they drove through the park.

The keeper was unaware that on those outings, the usually quiet elephant realised that the other animals were still allowed to live in the wild whereas, for most of the time it was now kept indoors. It began to get very agitated, its agitation turned to frustration, its frustration turned to anger and eventually it decided to make a bid for freedom. In breaking loose it showed the keeper he was not the strong as the circus might have implied. Brushing him aside, it left him unconscious on the floor.

Charging across the park, the elephant crashed through a small wood. When it emerged its curled trunk was holding aloft a branch it had torn from a young tree. Its small eyes were open wide and its ears were flapping as it ran. At one point it veered towards two giraffes, but the giraffes' legs were as long as their necks and they quickly galloped away. A short distance farther on a herd of zebras caught its attention, but they also were more fleet-of-foot and quickly scattered.

At that stage the elephant must have realised that these animals were on the other side of a fence. Turning away from them, it spotted the pride of lions that were lying around the earth and, discarding the branch, lowered its trunk and charged them. The lions moved aside, but only far enough to avoid being trampled by its huge feet. Not to be outdone, the enraged elephant turned and lunged at them again. This time, even the leader of the pride had to give way. For some reason the elephant followed it and even though it snarled and pawed the air in an act of defiance it had no option but to back away. At this stage the lioness decided to withdraw from the scene and led the cubs back to the rise where they usually spent much of their time lying around waiting for food.

The foxes who had taken refuge below ground had no idea what was happening. To add to their fears they heard something heavy pounding the ground above them and felt the earth tremble. All they could do was sit tight, but when all was quite again Running Fox ventured to the entrance. To his surprise, he found that the earth was no longer beset by the big cat and immediately informed the others that the way was clear.

Black Tip was delighted to see his friends emerging from the earth and told the old fox, 'They're out.' He barked loudly to them to let them know where he was, and a moment later added, 'They're coming this way.'

'And where's the animal with the long nose?' added the old fox.

'It's still trying to chase one of the cats, but it's refusing to run.'

Small as the eyes of the elephant were, it spotted the foxes running away and, realising that the lion wasn't afraid of it, turned to chase them.

'It's coming after them,' Black Tip added.

'You mean the cat?'

'No. The animal with the long nose.' Feeling the old fox getting to his feet, he assured him, 'But it's slowing down. It'll never catch them.' Moments later, he whispered, 'They're almost here.'

By this stage the elephant had slowed to an ungainly trot, while the foxes were speeding across the lawn.

Running Fox arrived first and as the others tumbled in after him, he panted, 'Through the gates. Hurry, we can hide among the buildings.'

To their consternation they found that Nightshade wasn't with them, and when they looked back saw that she had stopped on the lawn. Almost as if she had forgotten that they were being pursued, she was hopping up and down on the short grass. While the fox is descended from the dog, it sometimes behaves like a cat and the others knew from the way she acting that she was pouncing in an effort to dislodge a worm or a mouse she had detected beneath the lawn.

How Nightshade could hear the sound of something so small and ignore the sound of something as big as the animal that was now bearing down on her, the others couldn't imagine. Nor could they understand what followed.

The elephant came stomping across the lawn, and when it reached Nightshade it stopped, raised its trunk above its head and trumpeted loudly. Nightshade, however, seemed unafraid. She just stood and stared up at the elephant which lowered its trunk until it was almost touching the ground and stared down at her.

At the same time, a long-tailed field mouse popped up out of a small hole to find out what had shaken its small underground home. Seeing that it had surfaced under the very nose of a fox, it knew it wouldn't make it back to its nest and decided to make a run for it. When it did it found itself facing an even bigger foe, one with much bigger ears than the fox that had heard it beneath the ground.

Normally, a fox hunting in this way would have pounced on the mouse, but this situation was far from normal. Nightshade just sat back and continued to stare at the elephant. Trapped between the two, the mouse had no option but to do the same. The great animal lifted one of its mighty feet to squash it. Desperately it looked around for a way of escape. It feared that if it turned back the fox would kill it, and if it went forward the elephant would kill it. Then it saw the two holes in the elephant's trunk and wondered if they might offer a way of escape.

Whether the huge creature was getting some strange vibes from Nightshade, or realised what the mouse was thinking, the foxes who watched this strange encounter couldn't tell. All they knew was that the creature raised its long nose high above its head, trumpeted loudly, turned and ran back into the farmyard.

The mouse immediately disappeared down the hole to the safety of its underground home, Nightshade ran over to the others and they all dashed in through the gates. Minutes later the keeper, who had just regained consciousness, ran over to the broken gates and, using all the strength he could muster, managed to pull them closed again. For the moment at any rate, they would keep the elephant in and the lions out.

Later, when Running Fox had led the others to safety, they wondered what had frightened the creature with the long nose. Had it been afraid of Nightshade? Or had it been afraid of the mouse? But why should it have been afraid of either of them? Old Sage Brush, for all his wisdom, couldn't tell. Whatever the reason, it was an experience the elephant would never forget; nor would the foxes, and certainly not the mouse.

THIRTEEN

A SHOT IN THE DARK

A spell of relatively mild weather had given way to colder, frostier conditions and the foxes were lying up on a gorse-covered hillside. They would hunt when the wintry sun had melted the frost and their tracks would not be seen. Better still, they would hunt at night when the air would be cold and clear and the scents strong and easy to follow. In the meantime, they had plenty to talk about. This time it was not about the Hills of the Long Low Cloud. Nor was it about the giant ginger cats, the ponies with black and white stripes or the tall animals with the long necks and long legs that ran fast, but with an ungainly gait. It was about the huge lumbering animal with the big flapping ears and the long nose and what had frightened it.

'That was a very brave thing you did.' said Vickey.

Nightshade shrugged. 'I didn't do anything.'

'But you were very small, I mean, compared with it.'

'Not as small as the mouse.'

'Still, you were great to stand your ground,' said Black Tip. 'It was very big.'

'But its eyes were very small. I just looked it in the eye and told it to go away.'

'I didn't hear you,' said Vickey.

'Nor I,' added Old Sage Brush, 'and my hearing is better than most.'

'But it did. Its ears were very big.'

'Were you not afraid it would stamp on you?' asked Vickey.

'Yes, but I knew it would stamp on the mouse first.'

'Maybe it knew what you were thinking,' suggested Bluebell.

'Maybe it knew what the mouse was thinking,' replied Nightshade.

'And what was that?'

'That it might run up the holes in its nose.'

They all laughed and when Nightshade had gone over to lie beside her friend Bluebell, Vickey whispered to Black Tip, 'How did she know what the mouse was thinking?'

'I don't know. How did the animal with the long nose know what the mouse was thinking? How did it know what Nightshade was thinking?'

'It beats me,' Vickey confessed. 'But I think Nightshade

can say things, or sense things in a way that we can't.'

'A bit like Ratwiddle.'

'I suppose so. I mean, we can hear and see better than most, think better than most, pick up a scent better than most, but Nightshade seems to be able to do something else, something she didn't learn from us.'

'Where did Ratwiddle learn it?'

'I think it's just something he was born with.'

Black Tip nodded. 'Maybe Nightshade was born with it too – whatever it is.'

Running Fox, who had listened to this exchange, said nothing until it seemed the subject had been dealt with as far as it could be.

'I don't have time to think,' he told them. 'I just take off and run as fast as I can.'

Old Sage Brush, who was dozing nearby, nodded, saying, 'That I can understand.'

Shortly after that they came to Man's Place. It wasn't a big place like the one Old Sage Brush and his friends had been in on their first great journey. Nevertheless, they knew it could still hold dangers, and on the advice of the old fox they stopped in a small wood overlooking it until they could decide what to do. On the first visit to Man's Place they had been lucky to meet the little fox called Scavenger who guided them through it. There was no such fox to guide them through this one, so they watched and waited to see if it might be safe to go through it when night fell, or if it would be better to go around it.

The foxes were now on the outskirts of a small town, and towards dusk gulls began circling above the houses.

'I hear gok-goks,' remarked Old Sage Brush.

Looking down, they saw people leaving their wheelie bins out for their rubbish to be collected next day.

'Will we go down and topple one?' Nightshade asked Vickey, excited by the prospect of finding another container with something sweet in it.

'And show me how?' said Bluebell. 'When we tried to topple the beehive it didn't work.'

Vickey consulted Black Tip and Old Sage Brush, both of whom thought it too risky.

'But we did it before,' argued Nightshade.

'Where man lives in great numbers the risks may be greater,' said the old fox.

Seeing that Vickey was reluctant to go, Running Fox suggested, 'I could go with them and keep an eye on them.' When the others didn't reply he added, 'Where man lives in great numbers he doesn't keep hens, so we are not a threat to him.'

'He may not have hens,' said Vickey, 'but he has dogs. and they can be a threat to us.'

'The kind of dogs man keeps around his place don't run very far,' Running Fox told them. 'If Bluebell and Nightshade can outrun the giant ginger cat, they can outrun any mongrels we might meet down there. Anyway, I'm sure the local foxes will have left out messages for one another if there is any danger.'

That seemed to satisfy Old Sage Brush and he agreed to let them go, but only as far as the edge of Man's Place.

Black and Vickey Tip didn't argue the point, but they had certain reservations which they didn't want to voice in front of the old fox. Man's mongrels, they knew, might not pose a problem for Running Fox, but when travelling with Old Sage Brush before they had found that such dogs could run fast and bite deep. Taking Running Fox aside, they told him of their concerns. However, he assured them he would be careful not to bring any danger upon them.

When darkness fell, Bluebell and Nightshade saw lights come on in Man's Place and shadowy figures moving around his pathways. They were impatient to be on their way, but Running Fox told them they must wait until darkness closed in around Man's Place again and he was no longer to be seen.

The two of them thought the time to go would never come. Then the lights in the houses began to go out. There was still some light coming from the pathways beyond, but that didn't seem to worry Running Fox. When the last light in the houses went out, he got up and told them to follow him. Vickey warned them to be careful and off they went.

The back gardens of the houses faced the fields, and when

they reached the end house Running Fox stopped and listened. All was quiet. The light from the pathways beyond barely reached them, and if man was still up and about, he didn't see them as they stole past the side of the house to where a wheelie bin had been left on the pavement.

When Bluebell looked up at the bin she could smell its contents. It was a bad smell, strong too. In fact, she found it repulsive, and wondered how something so awful could provide them with a container of sweetness like the one Nightshade had told her about.

Nightshade immediately jumped up on to the bin, put her front paws on the handles and told Bluebell to do the same. Running Fox, who was keeping an eye out for any danger, watched as they began to rock the bin back and forth. Moments later it toppled over and he had to step smartly out of the way as the contents came spilling out on to the pathway. Nightshade and Bluebell immediately began to forage for the food they could smell among the rubbish. In the house nearby, a dog began to bark, and Running Fox told them to hurry.

Bluebell was about to go, when Nightshade assured her, 'It's all right. It's inside.'

'It's not all right,' Running Fox told her. 'Come on. Run.'

When Vickey and Nightshade had toppled a bin, the fact that the dog was in the house and not rambling around it had given them time to get food from the rubbish and still get away. As a result, Nightshade felt she could delay just that little bit longer this time. It was only a few seconds, but in the world of the fox a few seconds can mean the difference between life and death.

A light went on and a door opened. Nightshade and Bluebell finally responded to Running Fox's warning, and took off the way they had come. Behind them, the dog came bounding out of the house followed by a man. The dog was still barking and the man was swearing. But it wasn't just a few swear words that were aimed at the foxes. As they fled from the rim of light, sparks split the darkness with the sound of thunder. A hail of lead pellets whizzed past them and ricocheted off the street with a singing sound of a near miss. A second shot followed, and they heard the same singing sound close behind. They put on a spurt and when they reached the field they heard several more shots. All came in quick succession – shots in the dark, fired in the hope that one just might find its mark.

There were no more shots, but now Bluebell and Nightshade could hear the dog speeding after them. Running Fox, they knew, was a short distance ahead of them and having followed him in their flight from the giant ginger cat, they did what he would have wanted without being told. They split up and when the dog came to the place in the field where they had done so, it stopped, wondering which way to go. It sniffed around until it was confused. Then it returned to the house, where its master patted it on the head saying it was a good dog, and cursed the foxes that had become such a nuisance.

Vickey and Black Tip had been scanning Man's Place from the nearby hill and were anxiously awaiting the return of their friends when they heard the shots. The location of the flashes confirmed that the three had encountered a shooter. The barking also indicated that a dog had taken up the chase. Fortunately, there was no squeal of pain to suggest that the pellets had found their mark; no excitement in the bark of the dog to suggest it had found a fox. But if the three made it back, the dog might be on their heels. The old fox got up. It was time to go.

They were about to leave when Running Fox arrived, followed by Bluebell. Running Fox assured them they could relax as the dog had given up the chase. However, there was no sign of Nightshade, and as time passed it became obvious that she wasn't about to join them.

By this time Bluebell had lowered her head on to her front paws and was bemoaning the fact that her friend had not returned. 'It's all my fault,' she cried. 'If I hadn't asked her to show me how to do it, she would still be alive.'

Vickey tried to console her, saying, 'It was her idea to go, not yours. And maybe she is still alive. Maybe there's another reason why she hasn't come back.'

'It's my fault,' Running Fox said.' I was supposed to be

looking after them.'

'You were looking after us,' Bluebell told him, 'but we didn't run when you told us too. It's all my fault.'

'I said you could go,' said Old Sage Brush. 'So you could say it was my fault.'

'Were there any messages left out to warn you there might be danger?' Black Tip asked Running Fox.

'No – none that I could detect.'

'Then it's the fault of the foxes who live down there. When there are shooters around, we always warn others.'

'I wonder why they didn't tell us?' asked Vickey.

'Only they can answer for that,' said the old fox.

'Anyway, we know now,' said Running Fox, 'and I'm going to go back down there and find out what's happened to Nightshade.'

Before the others could say anything, he was gone.

When Running Fox reached the houses he stayed well clear of the one where the man had come out and shot at them. None of the houses differed from one another, nor did the gardens at the rear. At the end of each was a low wall, and close to the wall was a garden shed. The houses also had one other thing in common. From the time they had been built, they had provided a home not only for people but for the foxes who had come to depend on people.

However, all that had now changed, as Running Fox was soon to discover. He trotted quietly along the field, and when he was far enough away from the house of the shooter, hopped up on to the wall and dropped into one of the gardens. It was only then that he found the garden was occupied.

From the shadows another fox told him, 'This is my patch. Any food to be found here is mine.'

'I'm not looking for food,' Running Fox replied. 'I'm looking for a friend of mine. We were shot at earlier tonight and she has disappeared. I'm afraid she may have been injured.'

'There is an injured fox all right, farther along. But man is not friendly there either and you may find the foxes that live there even less so.'

Running Fox was puzzled, not by the fact that man might not be friendly – that was something he always took for granted – but by the suggestion that the other foxes might not be willing to help him. He was tempted to ask why, but was now more anxious than ever to find Nightshade. If she was injured, and if the local foxes had not come to her aid, it was important that he should locate her as soon as possible.

The warning given by first fox turned out to be well-founded. In each and every garden Running Fox passed through, he got one message and one message only from the foxes who lived there: he was not welcome and should keep going. Their one concern seemed to be that he should not hunt for food in their patch. Furthermore, they appeared to be unconcerned about the fact that an injured fox might be lying up somewhere nearby and in need of food or other assistance. So where was Nightshade, he wondered, and how was he to find her?

Anxious though he was not to draw man's attention to his presence, Running Fox decided there was only way to locate her. He hopped back over the wall and when he was some distance out in the field, he called her. No doors opened this time, no shots sounded, but there was no answering call. As he sat back and wondered what to do, he suddenly found Black Tip beside him.

'What's going on?' whispered Black Tip.

'It's very strange,' Running Fox told him. 'The foxes in there seem to be closer to man than they are to us. They know Nightshade has been injured, but they're not at all bothered about it.'

'Did they say where she might be?'

'No. I tried calling her but there was no reply. Why don't you try? Your call might be more familiar to her.'

No sooner had Black Tip's call died away than there was an answering call from one of the gardens.

'At least we know she's still alive,' said Black Tip. 'You go back and tell the others. I took pellets out of Vickey once when she was shot. Maybe I can do the same for Nightshade.'

As Running Fox raced back up to the wood, Black Tip cautiously made his way into the garden where Nightshade's answering call had come from, and found her waiting for him in an earth beneath a shed.

'Nightshade,' he panted. 'I thought we would never find you. Bluebell is sick with worry. So are the others. When you didn't return we thought you had been shot.'

'I'm fine,' she assured him. Then, pointing with her nose to another fox who was lying nearby, added, 'But he isn't in great shape.'

Black Tip crept closer to the other fox. He could see its head was raised to look at him. Or had its head already been raised?

'Ratwiddle!' he exclaimed. When there was no response he asked Nightshade, 'How did you know he was here?'

'I just knew.'

'Is he badly injured?'

'Badly enough. He got it in the hip.'

Black Tip looked at the wound. 'I need to clean it. But I think you'd better talk to him while I do so – try and take his mind off it.'

Black Tip cleaned Ratwiddle's wound as gently as he could and removed some pellets that clung to his torn flesh. Now and then Ratwiddle flinched but he didn't complain.

'Has he been here long?' asked Black Tip.

'Long enough,' said another voice from farther along the earth. 'He just staggered in here and lay down.'

'I take it then this is your earth?'

'My earth and my patch. You won't find any food here?'

Black Tip now realised he was talking to a vixen, and asked her, 'What's your name?'

'Man calls me Foxy.'

'Man!' exclaimed Black Tip.

'Of course. Here we live with man?'

'What do you mean, live with man?'

'We live under places like this where he keeps things for digging, even up on top of them when the weather is good. Some of us even live beneath the places where he lives whenever we can find a way in.'

'And where do you hunt?' asked Black Tip.

'We don't hunt. We don't have to. Man feeds us — or at least he used to.'

'You mean, like his dog?'

'No, we keep our distance until he leaves out food for us.'

'What kind of food?' asked Nightshade

'All kinds — food you would never have tasted in the wild.'

'I didn't come from the wild,' Nightshade told her, 'I was reared in a fur farm.'

'I doubt if you would have tasted it there either. Now, how would I describe it?' Foxy thought for a moment before going on to speak of flavours that had once been foreign to the fox but had become very enjoyable to those who lived with man. Some of it had a sharp tang, she said. Some of it was sweet, some of it was sour. Some of it left a dry taste, while some of it left a taste in their mouths that made them long for more.

Foxy, of course, couldn't put names on the different foods, but she did manage to give Black Tip and Nightshade a picture of the unusual diet enjoyed by the urban fox. They had, it appeared, developed tastes that mirrored the food favoured in different houses, much of it from takeaways. While one fox might have developed a taste for Chinese food, another had come to like Indian food. Among the different types of food they got were chicken curry, prawn curry, garlic bread, kebabs, spare ribs, hamburgers, onion rings, chicken wings, chicken korma, fish and chips, potato wedges, sushi, meat balls, chicken balls, pizzas, ketchup – even vegetarian food.

'Sounds a lot better than the food we were given in the fur farm,' Nightshade remarked.

'But I have seen no trace of this food anywhere,' said Black Tip.

Foxy lowered her head. 'That's because man has stopped giving us food – at least not food we can eat.'

'Why,' he asked. 'What happened?'

'I have only one cub left.' She gestured towards a side tunnel and they could just make out the form of a young fox. He was dozing and hadn't taken any interest in the visitors. 'He felt cornered and I'm afraid he bared his teeth at man when he was offering him food. Now man thinks we are dangerous. After that, the food he left out began to have a different taste. It made many of us sick. Some died, including my other three cubs. Others were caught in nets and taken away. Some, like your friend, have been shot.'

The foxes were unaware, of course, that the incident in which the young fox had bared his teeth was what man would have called the last straw, being only one of a long list of incidents that had made them a nuisance. High among these was the foxes' habit of digging small holes, and occasionally larger ones, in the lawns. These holes could be filled in relatively easily, but when the foxes began to dig such holes in their mini golf course, the townspeople decided it was time to get rid of them.

Foxy, of course, saw their problem only in the context of the incident with her cub and the consequent loss not only of her other cubs but of food.

Black Tip shook his head. 'I sympathise with you on the death of your cubs, and I don't wish to be unkind, but it seems to me that you – and the other foxes who live here – have chosen to eat like a dog and sleep like a dog. So, if one of you bites man when he feeds you, what else do you expect?'

'He didn't bite him,' said Foxy, 'but maybe now you understand why we cannot share our food with you or with your friend who lies here injured – we haven't got any.'

'Have you not tried rabbit?' asked Black Tip.

'Rabbit?' said Foxy. 'I don't think man eats rabbit.'

'So if he doesn't eat rabbit, you don't eat rabbit?'

'Where else would we get it?'

'There are rabbits in the fields. If your cub has caused this problem, why don't you send him out to hunt for them?'

'Hunt? He doesn't know how.'

Black Tip was incredulous. 'He doesn't know how to hunt?'

'I told you, the foxes who live here don't have to hunt. I have never shown any of my cubs how to hunt — there was no need to.'

'Well, if what you tell me is true, there is a need to hunt now.'

'It's not food Ratwiddle needs,' Nightshade said. 'He wants something to heal his wound.'

'So he can speak — that's a good sign.' Black Tip edged closer, saying, "Ratwiddle, this is your friend Black Tip. We've come to help you. If there is something that will heal your wound, tell us what it is so that we can get it.'

When Ratwiddle made no reply, Nightshade lay down beside him and put her head to his. 'He says there is something. He speaks of the arching briar.'

'I didn't hear him,' said Black Tip.

'Nor I,' said Foxy.

Nightshade said no more and Black Tip asked Foxy, 'Are there any briars to be found here?'

'No. Man has cleared them away.'

'Then it is in the fields that we must look for them.'

'If you take my advice,' said Foxy, 'you will take him with you. It's too dangerous for so many to be here. If man hears us he will seek us out.'

Nightshade shook her head. 'I don't think he'll be able to walk.'

'If Hop-along can walk on three legs,' Black Tip told her, 'so can he. But we'll need help. You stay here with him and I'll go and get Running Fox.'

Before leaving, Black Tip looked back and told Foxy, 'You have given our friend refuge when you couldn't give him food. For that we are grateful. If you wish to come with us, we can hunt for something much tastier than anything you have eaten here.'

Foxy smiled. 'I won't. To tell you the truth, I've forgotten how. But my cub is fully grown now. Perhaps you might show him how to hunt.'

'What's his name?'

'Boney'

'All right. Make sure he's ready.'

'Boney?' said Nightshade when Black Tip had gone. 'Where did he get a name like that?'

'The others called him that when he was young because he was so thin. I suppose the name stuck. But where did you get a name like Nightshade?'

As they waited for Black Tip and Running Fox to come, Nightshade told Foxy about their escape from the fur farm where all the foxes were nameless, how they had been given names by Vickey and Old Sage Brush, and how they were being taught the ways of the wild on their journey to the Hills of the Long Low Cloud.

'This is the only world Boney has known,' said Foxy. 'I wonder what he'll think of the world out there?'

How Boney had survived the poisoned food that had been left out for him, was one of nature's mysteries. He could, of course, have tried to forage for himself, but didn't know how. And so he had continued to laze around in the hope that man might give him something more palatable. However, no more food, either good or bad, was forthcoming. Furthermore, he had reached the stage where his mother was unwilling or unable to provide for him. As a result he agreed, albeit reluctantly, to go with Black Tip and his friends.

With Nightshade's help, Black Tip and Running Fox managed to coax Ratwiddle on to his feet and stagger up to the wood.

'What are we going to do?' asked Vickey. 'We can't stay here. It will soon be daylight.'

'I don't think the dog was a hunting dog,' Bluebell recalled. 'It didn't chase us very far, so maybe it won't come looking for us.'

'Maybe not,' said the old fox, 'but the situation has changed. Ratwiddle's blood is on the grass and if dogs like that pick up the scent of it, they will know his weakness. Then *they* will be hunting dogs.'

Running Fox nodded. 'You're right. We must get him to an earth where he'll be safe.'

'Somewhere where we'll all be safe,' added Vickey.

'He told Nightshade there's something that will help him heal,' said Black Tip.

Nightshade nodded. 'It's something to do with the arching briar.'

'Well,' said Vickey, 'whatever it is, it'll take time for that wound to heal – I know.'

'But where will we go?' asked Black Tip.

'There's an earth not far distant from here,' said Running Fox. 'It's a bolt hole I use when I'm being chased by the howling dogs. As it so happens, it's protected by the arching briars. He'll be safe there – you'll all be safe there.'

The old fox nodded. 'And you'll be able to find it in the dark?'

Running Fox smiled. 'I could find it with my eyes shut.'

The old fox grunted. 'It's enough that I should have mine shut. Keep yours wide open and lead on. Hopefully Ratwiddle will be able to make it.'

FOURTEEN

THE FOX AND THE DECOY

The journey to the earth with the arching briar was a slow and tortuous one. Ratwiddle stumbled and fell many times. He was dragging his leg behind him and was obviously in great pain. Despite that, he never complained, but held his head high and kept going. Nightshade never left his side, assuring him there wasn't much farther to go. The others also helped him every way they could. The truth was there wasn't much they could do, but whenever he fell they let him rest as long as he needed and added their words of encouragement.

Their problem was compounded by the fact that Black Tip had to guide Old Sage Brush while one of them had to hang back and stay with Boney, who seemed unable or unwilling to keep up with them.

As the first streaks of dawn appeared in the cold blue sky, the others could see that the pain and the loss of blood were slowly draining the strength from Ratwiddle's injured body. His rest periods now became longer and their words of encouragement appeared to have less effect on him. Eventually he lay down and it seemed that he didn't have the will or the energy to get up again.

Not knowing what to do, Vickey lay down beside him. 'If the frost sets in on him,' she told the others, 'he'll die. We must keep him warm.'

They all lay down around him to give him what heat and words of support they could. His head, which was normally raised as if he was looking up at the sky, now lay on the grass, and as they listened to his heavy breathing and watched his body heave, they knew he was unlikely to make it.

'We're all trying to talk to him at the same time,' said Old Sage Brush. 'Maybe he can't make out what we're saying. Nightshade, why don't you try and talk to him – on your own, and in your own way?'

The old fox moved away a short distance and the others followed.

'You think she might talk to him the way she talked to the animal with the long nose?' asked Vickey.

'Hopefully.'

'But that animal had big ears,' Black Tip recalled.

'We also have big ears,' the old fox reminded him.

'But we didn't hear her speak to the animal with the big ears,' said Black Tip. 'Maybe it was the mouse that frightened it.'

'We never heard Nightshade speak to Ratwiddle,' said Vickey. 'Yet she was able to tell us what he said.'

'What I hear, I see with my mind's eye,' the old fox told them, 'and from what you have told me it appears that Nightshade and Ratwiddle are of like minds. Perhaps in their case the mind's eye is more important than the size of the ear.'

Bluebell who was listening was confused. Whether the old fox was talking about the ear or the eye she couldn't quite understand. For her part, Nightshade seemed oblivious to what they were saying. As they stood aside and talked, she shuffled closer to Ratwiddle so that her nose was close to his. She didn't say anything, but after a short time it seemed to those who watched that she was somehow communicating with him.

Suddenly Ratwiddle's body twitched. Surprised, the others jumped back.

'What's happening?' asked Old Sage Brush.

Ratwiddle's body twitched again and he raised his head a little.

'It's working!' Vickey told the old fox. 'Whatever's going on, it's working. He's responding to Nightshade.'

A short time later Ratwiddle managed to get up and, with Nightshade by his side they slowly made their way to the place where Running Fox had his bolt hole. Alongside a ditch that was covered with a mass of bushes, hawthorns and brambles ran a small stream and they followed him along this until they reached the strong arching briars of a wild rose, or as man sometimes calls it, a dog rose. However, it was a place where neither man nor the howling dogs could follow.

Taking care to avoid the sharp spines of the briars, Running Fox led them up under a tangle of undergrowth so thick they had to lower themselves until their bellies were touching the ground and creep. Ratwidde had to lie on his side and scrabble forward dragging his injured leg, over which he has lost all control. It was a process that must have caused him unimaginable pain, but Nightshade kept him going, nosing his injured leg forward and sometimes pushing him with her head. The others helped her and bit by bit they got him into the earth. There they made him as comfortable as they could and tried to assure him that he was going to be all right. Vickey cleaned his wound but it began to bleed again and they knew it would take more than a secure earth and comforting words to make him better.

Once again, however, they had not reckoned on the strange affinity Nightshade had with Ratwiddle.

'You said there was something that could heal his wound,' said Vickey. 'Something about the arching briar. Do you know what it is?'

'Yes, it's the leaf.'

Black Tip shook his head. He hadn't heard Ratwiddle say anything, and yet Nightshade, who had lived in a cage, knew about a leaf that could heal.

Seeing the bewildered look on his face, Nightshade added. 'Really. Ratwiddle told me.'

Vickey nodded. Ratwiddle, they believed, had got a strange sickness from hunting rats among the gnarled roots of the willows down by the lake in the Land of Sinna. It was the same sickness, they knew, that had left him with the stiff neck so that he was always looking up at the sky. Perhaps he had used the leaf of the arching briar to heal his wounds whenever he had been bitten. Perhaps ... There was so much about Ratwiddle they didn't understand. He was such a loner and seemed to know things no other foxes knew... even things that hadn't happened and were going to happen.

'Okay,' said Vickey, 'let's get some.'

Emerging from the earth, Vickey looked up at the long arching briars of the dog rose. Its great hooked spines remained strong and sharp and would catch on any dog that looked for the secret way into Running Fox's earth, but its leaves had long since gone. So also had its five-petal pink and white roses. Similar roses had had been used as symbols of kings and queens since medieval times. However, it was to the king of the trees that Nightshade turned – the lesser and more humble bramble. While the bramble loses many of its leaves in winter, it doesn't lose them all and when Nightshade and Vickey found one farther along the hedge, they reached up to pluck some of the leaves that still clung to it. Fortunately, the thorns on the bramble were much smaller than the spines on the dog rose. On warmer days Vickey and her friends had enjoyed a change of diet by picking its black berries and now she showed Nightshade how to pluck a mouthful of leaves without drawing blood.

When they returned they found that Ratwiddle was still bleeding. Almost as if he was somehow telling Nightshade what to do, she crushed the leaves she had gathered and gently put them on his hip.

Vickey did likewise, saying, 'It'll take time, but let's hope it'll work.'

Nightshade lay down beside Ratwiddle again and put her nose to his. The others said no more, but still they wondered how she – or Ratwiddle – could have known about the bramble leaves. They would have wondered even more had they known that man had once used a poultice of crushed leaves from the bramble to ease the pain of burns and insect bites and to stop bleeding caused by the thorns when picking blackberries.

'Now,' said the old fox, 'I don't know about the rest of you, but I'm hungry. And from what you tell me, I gather young Boney here hasn't eaten for even longer.'

It was clear that Nightshade wasn't prepared to leave Ratwiddle's side, even for food. Bluebell agreed to stay and keep her company and so, leaving Running Fox to keep an eye on them all, Black Tip and Vickey set off with a reluctant Boney in tow.

The frost had melted in a weak mid-day sun, and some rabbits, they discovered, were taking advantage of it. The rabbits had made their burrows in a dry ditch beneath a hawthorn hedge. Some were hopping around the entrance to the burrows, while others were nibbling at the grass farther out. Feeling Boney quiver at the sight of them, Vickey told him to be still and keep quiet.

'Why don't we rush them?' he whispered.

'Because they'll be back in their burrows before we get near them. Leave it to Black Tip. He'll show you how to catch them.'

Nevertheless, it was all Vickey could do to keep Boney from rushing straight in. Only the promise of a share in what they would catch made him lie down beside her and watch.

Inexperienced as he was in the ways of the wild, Boney couldn't imagine how any fox could get near the rabbits without being seen. Black Tip had slipped away and wasn't even in the same field as the rabbits. But then, he discovered, that was the ploy. Suddenly Black Tip came crashing across the top of the ditch from the other field. The rabbits were cut off and immediately scattered. Black Tip caught one of them and before Boney knew what was happening, Vickey had dashed forward and caught another.

When the two returned with their catch, Boney wanted his share of it there and then, but learned another lesson – one the others had learned from Old Sage Brush.

'If we eat here,' Black Tip told him, 'man will read the signs and know we are in the area. That could draw a trapper upon us, or even the howling dogs.'

'And we are very vulnerable at the moment,' Vickey reminded him. 'Ratwiddle lies in the earth seriously injured and don't forget, Old Sage Brush is blind. We need food, but we also need time.'

Black Tip and Vickey picked up the rabbits they had caught and Boney followed them back to the earth. He was hungry, very, very hungry and he wished he was back at Man's Place. Man might not be leaving food out for them now, he thought, but there was always some morsel left after his mother had been foraging, and he didn't have to hunt for it, or wait to eat it. He also found that his share of the rabbits didn't amount to much. It certainly didn't satisfy his hunger and he was determined that he would return to the garden shed where his mother lived at the first opportunity.

Had it not been for the fact that Ratwiddle was asleep and Nightshade said she wasn't hungry, Boney would have got even less rabbit, but he brightened up when Old Sage Brush suggested that some of them should go out and hunt again.

'I enjoyed that,' he said to no one in particular, 'but it has only whetted my appetite.' He licked his lips and added, 'Maybe we can find something a little tastier.'

'Like what?' asked Boney.

'Who knows what the hedgerows hold beside rabbits?' replied the old fox. 'Not man's leftovers, I can assure you, but what nature has left for us. Black Tip, why don't you take Boney out again and show him what I mean. And Running Fox, perhaps you and Bluebell could do the same. Vickey can keep me company and help Nightshade in her vigil with Ratwiddle.'

It was now late afternoon and the frost was beginning to make the grass crisp and white again. For many of the birds and animals of the fields it was time to find cover, but for the four foxes who slipped out of the earth beneath the arching briar, it was a good time for hunting.

Running Fox led Bluebell across the fields to an area of woodland and scrub where he had hunted before. The air was sharp and fresh and when they sniffed it, they got a variety of scents. Rabbits were now in their burrows and there was only a faint trace of their presence on the flattened ground outside. Then came the stronger scent of a hare, probably from a den in one of the clumps of withered grass out in the middle of the field. But it was something else they were after. Somewhere in the scrub, they knew, pheasants would have settled in for the night.

In her journey towards the Hills of the Long Low Cloud, Bluebell had been taught by Old Sage Brush and his friends how to distinguish one scent from another, and when she told Running Fox that she had detected the scent of a pheasant, he told her, 'You have learned well. Why don't you see if you can sniff it out?'

'But this is your hunting ground, not mine,' she replied.

Running Fox smiled. 'When the howling dogs are hunting here, it's their hunting ground. When I'm hunting here it's mine. But tonight it's ours. Find the pheasant and we'll hunt it together.'

Bluebell nosed around the edge of the scrub and found the splayed tracks of a pheasant in mud that was beginning to harden. Her long ears twitched this way and that, but she heard nothing and realised that if the pheasant sat tight, its exact location would be difficult to pinpoint.

Running Fox watched approvingly as she deliberately made her presence known to the pheasant by moving some of the scrub aside. The pheasant, he knew, would hear her and perhaps rise a little, ready for flight. And it did. It made a sound so slight that only the ears of a fox could pick it up. It also gave off a stronger scent.

Now Bluebell knew exactly where the pheasant was. With a glance at Running Fox to let him know what she was about to do, she charged in. Before she could grab the pheasant, it burst into flight, crashing up and out with a raucous call of alarm and a loud flap of its wings. The pheasant, of course, was unaware that another fox was waiting, and before it could gain enough height, Running Fox gave a great leap and brought it down.

When Bluebell emerged from the scrub and saw the pheasant lying at his feet, she smiled, saying, 'Well done. I just missed it.'

'No you didn't,' he said. 'You flushed it out.'

'But you caught it.'

'Yes, but it's your catch, so you carry it back.'

Bluebell could see from its dark green head and white collar that it was a cock pheasant. It was also quite heavy and she had to hold it tightly. She also held her head high, not only to keep its long brown tail from dragging along the ground, but because she was proud of the way she had hunted in front of Running Fox about whose exploits she had heard so much. She also wondered how Black Tip and Boney were doing.

Unlike Bluebell, Boney was not a willing learner. The thought of more food did appeal to him but the prospect of having to catch it did not. It was with great reluctance, therefore, that he followed Black Tip and it wasn't long before he began to think they would never get to wherever they were going. Why, he wondered, couldn't Black Tip just go over to a hedge and get another rabbit the way he had done before. Now he seemed to be more interested in looking up at the sky? Why, he couldn't imagine. There was nothing up there that he could see, and even if there was, he reckoned a fox would need wings to catch it.

Black Tip told Boney in no uncertain terms not to be lagging behind and to keep close. Other than that, he didn't feel inclined to tell him anything. If he had asked where they were going, or even shown an interest in hunting, he would have told him, but the young fox from Man's Place hadn't even bothered to talk to him.

To get something different for Old Sage Brush, something a little tastier, Black Tip was seeking out the nearest river and when, eventually, he did find one he followed it until he came to a lake. There, he hid among the rushes at the edge of the water and told Boney to do the same. The light was beginning to fade now, and the blue of the sky was hardening into a purple that signalled a night of even harder frost. Boney fidgeted and wondered what they were waiting for. Black Tip told him to be still and looked up at the sky. Boney did the same, but again, saw nothing. Finally, he asked, 'What are you looking up there for?'

'Ducks,' Black Tip replied.

'But if they are up there, how are we going to catch them?'

Black Tip shook his head. How, he wondered, could a fox be so foolish? 'We're not going to catch them up there! They come down to the edge of the water to settle for the night, and when they do we'll be waiting for them.'

Just then a flock of teal sped down across the lake, turned and landed on a small muddy island. A short time later, several mallard flew in and swooped overhead but didn't land. Seeing them, Boney made to rise, but Black Tip bade him be still. 'Listen,' he whispered.

Boney listened, but didn't hear anything.

'Lie still,' Black Tip whispered. 'Man is also after the ducks – look.'

Boney now saw several men approaching the lake shore. They were carrying shotguns, but it didn't bother him. Where he came from he was used to man's presence. After all, it was man who had fed him for most of his young life. One man, he knew, had shot at foxes in a garden some distance away. But he had never seen that man. Nor had he ever seen a gun.

The shooters had been lying in wait for the ducks farther down the lake, and when they saw them flying low over another the part of the shore, decided that was where they would have the best chance of a shot. They were unaware, of course, that foxes were also waiting there for the ducks.

As the shooters moved into position not far from them, Black Tip warned Boney once again to lie still. 'If you don't, it'll be us they'll be shooting, not the ducks!'

However, Boney was difficult to restrain and Black Tip felt him quivering when one of the shooters crept forward. He had a duck in his hand, and even in the fading light its colours were all too familiar to Black Tip – just as they would be to other ducks. It had all the colours he had seen on the mallard drake – yellow, green, white, brown, grey, blue. All, that is, except one. It didn't have orange-coloured legs. In fact, it had only one leg, a straight one that the man pushed into the mud.

When the man retreated to his hiding place he lay down and, taking a duck-caller from his pocket blew on it several times. Then he and his friends waited in the hope that some mallard would hear what they thought was the call of another duck, see the decoy and be tempted to land within range of their guns.

Having been reared in a back garden, Boney didn't know the difference between a real duck and a decoy. As far as he was concerned, man was leaving out food for him. Before Black Tip could stop him, he dashed over to the decoy, caught it by the white ring on its neck and ran away from the lake as fast as his legs could carry him.

If Black Tip was startled by Boney's action, the duck hunters were astonished. Seeing the fox race off with their decoy in his mouth they scrambled to their feet, but by the time they had fired at it, it was too late. Boney was gone and so was their decoy. Out on the lake, a flock of mallard that had been seeking a suitable landing place, turned sharply at the sound of the shots, soared back up again and disappeared into the darkening sky.

Realising now that they were wasting their time, the

hunters turned and headed for home. What, they wondered, would the fox do with a plastic duck? Black Tip wondered the same thing, for he knew it was not a real duck. And had the decoy not been weighted to keep it firm in the mud, Boney might have wondered about it too. But he didn't. Hard and all as it felt, the weight told him it was food.

When the shooters related the story of the fox and the decoy their friends laughed, and on reflection, they laughed too. Back in the earth beneath the arching briar, Old Sage Brush and his friends also laughed. Needless to say, Black Tip would have preferred to bring home a duck – a real duck – rather than a story of a missed opportunity. Nevertheless, the story lifted the hearts of his friends for whom hunger was only one of their worries. And as Old Sage Brush pointed out, the night was young, the shooters had departed and they could now hunt without fear of man.

The task fell to Black Tip and Running Fox again. Running Fox had not forgotten the scent of hare he had detected before deciding to concentrate on the pheasant. The frost had taken a firm grip of the fields now, and like the pheasant, the hare was reluctant to leave its den. With Black Tip's help, Running Fox caught it and while duck might have been more to the liking of Old Sage Brush, the hare provided a more substantial meal for all of them. All, that is, except Ratwiddle. To their great relief, he was showing signs of life. He opened his eyes and raised his head, but it was as much as he could do and quickly went to sleep again.

As the others munched away, Vickey said, 'Boney is going to be disappointed when he finds there is no meat on that duck.'

'You can't help those who won't help themselves,' the old fox replied.

Black Tip nodded. 'There was no meeting of minds there.'

'At least Bluebell and Nightshade wanted to learn the ways of the wild,' said Vickey. 'Snowflake too. I think Boney is just bone lazy.'

The others laughed, and Old Sage Brush added, 'A clever fox who hunts well will survive well. Even a clever fox who is lazy. But a foolish fox who is lazy will not survive for long – at least, not in the wild.'

'It's a foolish fox who doesn't know how to hunt,' said Running Fox. 'Even Foxy doesn't seem to know how, or doesn't want to know.'

'So how are Foxy and her friends going to survive now that man has stopped feeding them,' Vickey wondered.

The old fox wiped his mouth with his paw. 'Oh, I have no doubt they'll survive.' He paused before adding. 'You see, it seems to me that those who depend on man have become a different breed of fox, quite unlike us who live in the wild. And somehow I think Foxy may not be as foolish as we might imagine.'

Nightshade, who had been pre-occupied with Ratwiddle,

now joined in the conversation. 'She didn't think it worth her while to warn us about the shooters – and look what happened to poor Ratwiddle.'

The old fox corrected her. 'Not shooters – shooter. There was only one, and I get the impression he was not a hunter. Ratwiddle was probably just in the wrong place at the wrong time. You know the way he runs around with his head in the air.'

'You're right,' said Running Fox. 'The shooter was not a hunter, and his dog was not a hunting dog. He just came out of his place to shoot at us when he heard us tumbling that thing over.'

'Even so,' said Vickey, 'why didn't Foxy and her friends warn us about him?'

'They were probably hoping the shooting would frighten us away,' said the old fox.

'Why would they want to do that?' asked Nightshade.

'I think they knew that if we were shot at there, we wouldn't look for any other food discarded by man.'

'You mean, in those things, like the ones we toppled?' asked Bluebell.

'I'm sure Foxy and her friends know better than to start knocking those over. They've made a nuisance enough of themselves already.'

'Where then?'

Turning to Black Tip, the old fox said, 'Remember our

first journey, when we took a wrong turn and ended up at the Land of the Giant Ginger Cats? The little fox we met …'

'Scavenger.'

'That's right. When he took us through Man's Place, you told me you saw a dog. Now tell me again, what was it doing?'

Black Tip recalled that when Scavenger led them through Man's Place in the dead of night, they saw a mongrel scraping among bags of rubbish looking for food.

'That's right,' said Vickey. 'Man hadn't bothered putting it in the kind of things we toppled.'

The old fox nodded. 'It seems to me he had just dumped some of his rubbish. And no doubt he does the same where Foxy lives. The calls of the gok-goks should have told us that.'

'So, by allowing the shooter to take a shot at us,' Running Fox added, 'she hoped we would go back to the fields and not compete with her and her friends for food like that.'

'They would have to root around for it,' said Black Tip, 'but they would have it for themselves.'

Vickey smiled. 'So who's the clever fox now?'

'Well, I've never met her,' Old Sage Brush replied, 'but at a guess, I'd say Foxy.'

FIFTEEN

THE CLOUD LIFTS

A twig dropped from the sky and something in the carpet of withered leaves beneath a beech tree stirred. The leaves were the same colour as a fox who was sleeping there and had it not been for the twig that fell on his nose he would have slept for longer, unseen and undisturbed by either dog or man. But now he was awake. He could hear the cawing of rooks as they swirled around the treetops, and while he couldn't see them, the falling twig told him they were collecting material to rebuild their nests.

Old Sage Brush eased himself up, shook the leaves that clung to his coat and stretched to ease the aches from his body. Hearing nothing else in the vicinity but the rooks, he made his way along the hedgerows until he came to the earth beneath the arching briars. The other foxes who were gathered there were, he found, excited.

'He's awake,' Vickey told him. 'Ratwiddle's awake!'

Some of them had returned from their night's hunting to find that their friend had finally stirred from the slumber induced by the pain in his hip. With the help of the poultice of bramble leaves, the injury had begun to heal, just as his friend, Nightshade had predicted, but the pain in his tortured mind had been slower to heal. He had raised his head a time or two only for it to flop down again, even opened his eyes in a bleary sort of way, but only now had he said anything. It was barely a whisper and the others gathered around to hear, but couldn't make out what he was saying.

'He says the cloud has lifted,' said Nightshade who was lying with her head close to his.

'What does he mean by that?' asked Bluebell.

When Nightshade offered no more information, Vickey said, 'Who knows?'

'Maybe he means the cloud has lifted from his mind,' Old Sage Brush suggested.

'If that's the case,' said Running Fox, 'he could be back to his old self again before we know it.'

Black Tip nodded. 'Hopefully. And if I know Ratwiddle, he won't hang around. It will be time for him to go.'

'It will soon be time for all of us to go,' said the old fox.

'Do you think we should go with him?' asked Running Fox. 'Keep an eye on him.'

'No. Ratwiddle will go his way, and we will go ours. The time has come to go back to Beech Paw.'

'But we haven't reached the Hills of the Long Low Cloud,' said Black Tip. 'In fact, we haven't even seen them.'

'Maybe,' replied the old fox, and it seemed to the others that he was echoing what Ratwiddle had said, 'Maybe the cloud has lifted.'

'What about our friends?' Vickey asked him. 'We promised to take them to a place where they could have a new life, a place where they could find a mate and hunt without fear of the trapper.'

'Snowflake has already taken Fang as a mate and gone to find a new life.'

'I know,' she said, 'but what about Bluebell?'

Bluebell smiled. 'I'm going back to Beech Paw with you.'

'And I'm going with her,' said Running Fox, 'if that's all right.'

'Of course it is,' Vickey assured them, 'but what about Nightshade? And who's going to look after Ratwiddle?'

'I think Ratwiddle has found a like mind,' said the old fox. 'Don't you?'

Vickey went over to Nightshade and lying down beside her, asked, 'Do you want to come back with us, or are you going to stay with Ratwiddle?'

Nightshade smiled. 'I couldn't leave him – not now when he has asked me to stay.'

Vickey was about to remark that she hadn't heard him say anything, but changed her mind. It just reinforced what they had known all along. Ratwiddle and Nightshade were two of a kind.

'But there's no hurry,' the old fox added. 'And we needn't worry about the trapper. By all accounts, Hop-along has taken care of him.'

Later, when they had eaten and the old fox dozed off, Bluebell joined Nightshade by the side of Ratwiddle, while the other three adjourned to another part of the earth to chat among themselves.

'Vickey,' Black Tip whispered. 'You were wondering if the Hills of the Long Low Cloud really exist. What do you think now?'

'I don't know. As you said yourself, you'd think we'd have seen them by this stage.'

'But if they don't exist, what does Old Sage Brush mean when he says the cloud has lifted?'

Vickey shrugged. 'Maybe he means something else.'

'Like what?'

'If Ratwiddle is saying the cloud has lifted from his mind, maybe Old Sage Brush is saying it has lifted from other minds too.'

'Whose minds?' asked Running Fox.

'Well, when we set out with Bluebell and her friends, I suppose you could say their minds were clouded for they knew nothing of the ways of the wild. Maybe he means that cloud has lifted.'

Running Fox nodded. 'You could be right. I can see Blue-bell has learned a lot, and I'm sure she'll learn a lot more on the way back.'

'They've all learned a lot,' added Black Tip.

Running Fox got up. 'And I thought Ratwiddle had a strange way of saying things!'

'You should know the old fox by now,' said Vickey.

'That's true. Anyway, I'll go and check on Ratwiddle – see if Bluebell and Nightshade need any help.

When Running Fox had gone, Black Tip shuffled closer to his mate. 'So,' he said, 'you think the Hills of the Long Low Cloud are just something we imagined?'

Vickey smiled. 'We'll never know now, will we?'

★ ★ ★

While Old Sage Brush had said it would soon be time for them to go, it wasn't until Ratwiddle had recovered that he told Black Tip to lead the way once more. Bluebell, of course, was sad to leave Nightshade behind, but she comforted herself with the thought that her friend had found something in Ratwiddle that she would not have found in anyone else. And she herself was looking forward to spending more time with Running Fox on the journey back.

Black Tip was tempted to ask the old fox to explain what

he had said about the cloud having lifted, but didn't want to show his ignorance, so he held his tongue and decided that Vickey's explanation for their turn-around was probably the right one.

Had he asked, the old fox would probably have given him another reason for his decision to turn back at this particular time. As the crows were rebuilding their nests, it told him that the fields and hedgerows would soon be springing back to life. What better time to turn around and go back, he would have said, for they could relax and enjoy themselves as they went along.

In fact, this was something they soon came to appreciate themselves, for as they made their way through the fields small birds were singing and tiny buds were beginning to appear in the hedgerows. On the ditches beneath, primroses were unfurling in a splash of yellow before the new leaves put them in the shade. When that happened, they knew, the birds would lay and life would begin all over again.

These were things Old Sage Brush couldn't see, but he could hear the birds and feel the new growth beneath his paws. Later, as they passed through the woods he could also feel tall stalks of bluebells brushing against him and he remembered the splash of colour they always brought to the woodland.

It was the first time Bluebell had seen bluebells and she realised what a lovely name Vickey had given her. 'She said my fur was as blue as the flowers of the wood,' she told Running Fox. 'So it is,' he replied, and as she wandered among them, the blue of her fur blending here and there with the blue of the flowers, he marvelled at how beautiful a creature the fur farm had produced.

All too soon the flowers of the wood faded and Bluebell watched in wonder as leaves came on the trees, birds she had not seen before came swooping over the meadows, and creatures that had always hidden from them performed a frenzied dance in the open fields.

From the cover of the hedgerows, she saw hares standing on their hind legs and squaring up to one another in a way that seemed quite mad to her, and had she known it, to man, while nearer the hedgerows cock pheasants flew at one another, their claws sending clouds of small feathers into the air.

Bluebell suggested they run at the hares and take them by surprise, but Running Fox told her the hares would see them coming long before they could get near and easily outrun them. However, the sparring pheasants were closer. They were too intent on what they were doing and would not have time to fly. As a result it was the fox, not the strongest pheasant that decided the outcome of more than one encounter before the feathers had even settled on the grass.

One day as they rested on a sunny hillside overlooking a river, Bluebell looked up at the sky, saying, 'Something has scratched it.'

'Scratched what?' asked Running Fox.

'The sky,' she replied. 'Something has scratched it.'

When Running Fox looked up he saw white lines spanning the blue of the sky and as he and Bluebell watched, they seemed to get wider and wider. Vapour trails, man called them, emissions from planes that flew so high even the foxes couldn't see them. But what caused the white lines was not known to the creatures of the wild, and Bluebell asked, 'Do you think it was done by the Great White Fox?'

Running Fox smiled. 'I don't really know. But I do know there's a nest over there in the fields with the long grass.'

'How do you know that? You haven't even been there today.'

'No, but there's a bird up there in the sky that tells me so – listen.'

Bluebell cocked an ear and, sure enough she heard the high-pitched singing of a skylark as it climbed higher and higher into the blue.

'It's sings above its nest,' Running Fox explained.

'Then, why don't we go and see if there are any eggs in it?'

'We could – if we knew where it was.'

'But if it's singing above its nest we can see where it comes down.'

'Ah, but that's the problem. It lands somewhere else – just so we won't find it.'

Old Sage Brush, who was lying nearby, smiled. 'The bigger birds may not sing as well as the smaller ones, but their eggs are bigger and easier to find. Why don't you take her down to the meadow and let her find them for herself?'

The peewit, Bluebell discovered, couldn't sing at all and wasn't as smart as the skylark. Its nest was just a scrape in the ground, and there was little or no grass to cover its eggs. They were big and much the same colour as the soil, but while this might have concealed them from man, they weren't dark enough to fool the keen eyes that now searched them out in the meadow.

When they tired of peewits' eggs, Running Fox and Bluebell lifted one each and carried them back to Old Sage Brush. He wasted no time in cracking one open, and as he savoured its contents they lay in the sun and listened to the birds. The different birds, Bluebell noticed, had different songs and then she heard one cooing somewhere in the distance. It rose and fell, a soft lilting coo and she remarked, 'It's nice, isn't it?

'What is?' asked Running Fox.

'The cooing of the pigeon.'

'That's not a pigeon. That's a coo-coo.'

'Oh, I've never seen a coo-coo. What's it like?'

'I've never seen one either,' Running Fox admitted. 'But that's the sound it makes.'

Their ears twitched this way and that but they couldn't quite locate where the cooing was coming from.

Vickey and Black Tip joined them, and having heard part of what they had said, Vickey asked, 'What have you never seen?'

'A coo-coo.'

'It's a very secretive bird all right,' said Black Tip.

The old fox licked the shell of the second egg clean. 'Pity Ratwiddle isn't here. He'd tell you all about it.'

Vickey nodded. 'That's right. He told us about it, but at first we didn't know what he meant.'

'Which isn't surprising,' said Black Tip.

'Why, what did he say?' asked Running Fox.

'He said…' Vickey tried to remember, 'What was it now, Black Tip?'

'He said,' Black Tip recalled, 'the call of the coo-coo will float on the wind, and the eggs will float on the water.'

'It took as us a long time to figure it out,' Vickey said. 'When we heard the call of the coo-coo we tried to track it down, find out what kind of bird it was. Eventually we saw it gliding down to the reeds by the lake.'

'And that was when we figured out what Ratwiddle had said,' Black Tip added.

'It was like a hawk,' Vickey continued. 'But it wasn't swooping on any of the birds down there. In fact we saw it landing on the nest of a singing bird.'

'The nest was too small for it,' said Black Tip, 'and afterwards we found the eggs of the singing bird floating in the water.'

Running Fox and Bluebell were wondering if what they had been told could really be true, when the call of the coo-coo came floating on the wind again.

'Come on,' said Running Fox, 'let's go down to the river to see if we can find any of those eggs.'

If the two of them had doubted anything they had been told, their doubts were dispelled when they made their way in among the reeds. Just as Ratwiddle had predicted, they found several eggs floating on the water. They were very small, but after the peewits' eggs, were nice and sweet to finish off with.

The nest where the eggs had come from was high in the reeds, and the bird that had built it wasn't far away. Its calls – which had earned it the name of reed warbler – were too low to deter the foxes or indeed the bigger bird that had visited the nest. In any event, it was no longer interested in the eggs in the water, but the one large egg that now occupied its nest.

When Running Fox and Bluebell retreated from the reeds, the little bird returned to the nest to spread itself on the egg it mistakenly believed to be its own, and from afar they once more heard the soft haunting call of what man called the cuckoo.

'What a strange bird,' Bluebell remarked. 'I wonder why it doesn't build its own nest – or even look for a bigger one?'

'Probably too lazy,' replied Running Fox. 'But then, we sometimes use earths that have been dug by other foxes – even badger setts. So I suppose we can be lazy too if it saves us a lot of work.'

Old Sage Brush was amused when Bluebell returned and told him all the things she had seen, for it was as if she was a cub who had seen them for the first time. He had enjoyed the peewits' eggs, but much more to his liking were duck eggs and when Black Tip suggested they follow the river for a while, he readily agreed. He also had something else in mind, and when they heard the loud croaking of frogs, Bluebell was about to learn another secret of the wild.

Like hares and pheasants, the frogs, she discovered, had thrown caution to the wind and gathered in large numbers in a muddy pond not far from the river. It was another mating ritual that left them prone to various predators including otters and herons, but on this occasion it was the foxes who got there first.

Old Sage Brush and his friends had feasted on frogs before, but it was a whole new experience for Bluebell. Just as man in certain countries considers frogs' legs to be a delicacy, she considered them to be every bit as tasty as the eggs of the peewit and the reed warbler. They were not, she learned, something they would find every day, but something special and a nice change from rabbit.

As they continued their journey, the blossoms of the

whitethorn came and went, falling like snow upon the ditches and disappearing just as quickly. Winter was now well behind them and summer was on its way.

While Bluebell was young and full of energy, the same could not be said of Old Sage Brush. Nevertheless, the leisurely journey suited both of them. While he rested, she explored. Her curiosity knew no bounds and she left their chosen path at every opportunity to see the things that had suddenly come to life in a world of sun she had never seen before. Running Fox was always by her side and taught her all he knew. So did Vickey and Black Tip, while the old fox was always on hand to give advice.

However, a fox's life is full of challenge. As the old fox had once remarked, 'If you're not strong you must be clever,' and while they were all looking forward to being back in the Land of Sinna, they would have to overcome one more challenge before peace could return to the Valley of the Fox.

SIXTEEN

A STING IN THE TAIL

Hop-along and She-la had waited patiently for the return of their friends. As winter had turned to spring and spring to summer, they had begun to fear they might never return. They had seen the blossoms come upon the black-thorns where they had their den. But their friends hadn't come. They had seen the blossoms come upon the whiteth-orn. But still their friends hadn't come. The blossoms had come upon the elderberry, and still they waited. Then, when the hogweed had bloomed again, and they had all but given up hope, the hedgerows came alive with something else - news that their friends had at long last arrived.

It was a most joyful reunion, but one that had to wait as caution was always uppermost in their minds. So as not to draw the attention of man to Hop-along's earth, the new arrivals split up. Old Sage Brush made his way to the earth where the four hedges met, while Vickey took Running Fox and Bluebell down into the disused quarry and her den in the cave beneath the rocks. Black Tip alone slipped into the blackthorns to announce their arrival, and it wasn't until darkness had fallen that the others followed.

Hop-along and She-la were greatly relieved to see that they were alive and well. Snowflake, they knew, had gone with Fang to seek a new life together. Bluebell looked splendid in her summer fur, but where was Nightshade? A lot, they learned, had happened since they had abandoned their journey and turned for home. They listened with great interest as the others told them how they had outwitted the white mink with the aid of a tree cat, how they had escaped from the claws of the giant ginger cats with the help of the monster with the long nose, how Nightshade had survived her encounter with the same creature with the help of a mouse, and how they had got the better of the howling dogs with something as small as a bee.

It was with much amusement, of course, that Hop-along and She-la learned that their friends had been outwitted by Foxy; sadness to learn that Ratwiddle had been shot and relief that Nightshade had stayed behind to look after him.

Fascinating as these stories were, and even though she had played a part in them, it was Hop-along's paw that fascinated Bluebell. There was Hop-along minus a paw. And there, just above him, was the paw hanging from the root of a black-thorn bush. Somehow, in her mind's eye, she couldn't connect the two.

Seeing her looking at one and then the other, Vickey said, 'But what about you, Hop-along? I see you have your paw back.'

Hop-along smiled. 'Better here than on the trapper's neck!'

'How did you get it back?' asked Black Tip. 'We heard you had got the better of him. But, tell us more.'

They all gathered round and Old Sage Brush nodded with satisfaction as Hop-along told them how he and She-la had lain in wait for the trapper and sprung a trap of their own. It was, they agreed, a wonderful story, for what the two of them had done required great cunning and courage. Considering Hop-along's handicap, it was something that matched, perhaps even excelled, anything they had done.

Since then, Hop-along added, the trapper and his dog had ceased to walk the fields in the valley and his traps were no more.

Unknown to the foxes, the fall on the rock had left the trapper with his own handicap. As a result, they were free to roam the Land of Sinna in a way they had never been able to do before.

When the grain crops ripened they turned the valley's fields from green to gold and the harvest provided a rich bounty for all. The farmers gathered up the grain and the foxes gathered up the rats and mice that had fed on the grain. Down near the lake, creamy meadowsweet spread its own colour of gold across another hunting ground. It was a marsh that Black Tip and his friends had once shared with Ratwiddle and now shared with Bluebell.

Higher up the valley, the hedgerows were intertwined with honeysuckle and a web of weeds through which the foxes could come and go as they wished and behind which they could rest when their bellies were full. From such a hiding place, Bluebell watched soft stars of thistledown drifting up from the meadows and she was happy, for the Land of Sinna was everything she had dreamed it would be.

However, the presence of a blue fox in the valley hadn't gone unnoticed, and it wasn't long before it became apparent that a different kind of trapper was at work.

It was Black Tip who spotted the problem first. He had more reason than most to be cautious when following a fox path through a hedge, being mindful of the time he had caught his neck in a choking trap. What he came across now, however, was different. It was a fine net like the one the trapper had used to catch Snowflake.

'I thought you said he no longer laid traps for us?' said Vickey.

'He doesn't,' Hop-along replied. 'Not since he fell and hit his head on the rock.'

In the days and nights that followed, they no longer felt

free to roam the fields and abandoned all of their earths in favour of the one in the blackthorns. They watched the pathways through the hedgerows to avoid the nets and they watched the man who was putting them there. The nets were difficult to see, they were so fine, but the man who put them there was easier to see. Unlike the trapper, he was fat and didn't seem to be a man of the fields. When he made his way through the hedgerows, he was clumsy, tearing his clothes and, judging by the noises he made, sometimes his hands. None of them had ever seen him before – none that is, except Bluebell. When she saw him, she began to shiver.

'What is it?' asked Vickey.

'It's him,' she whimpered.

'Who?'

'The man who kept us in the cages.'

Startled, the others asked what she meant as she and her friends from the fur farm had spoken of several men.

'When we were in the cages he was always walking around, looking at us. He was the one who pointed at us, telling the others which of us should be taken away and which of us should stay. It's me he's after.'

Bluebell was right. The man whose fur farm had been raided by the animal rights people had abandoned his farm but not his wish to produce more furs for the fashion industry. Having escaped from the clutches of the authorities, he had set up a new farm in another valley and was still in the process of building up his breeding stock. The blue fox would be a valuable addition to that stock, but the problem was how to catch it. His expertise lay in producing exotic colours of foxes, not in trapping the common red ones. However, the trapper of the red foxes had now retired, leaving him with no option but to try and catch the blue one himself.

'He's going to take me away and put me in a cage again,' Bluebell cried.

'Not if we can help it,' asserted Running Fox. 'Don't worry, you're safe here.'

'Running Fox is right,' Hop-along assured her. 'The trapper could never get in here to set any of his traps. The thorns are too sharp.'

Old Sage Brush, who had been listening, asked. 'Where else did you go where the trapper couldn't follow?'

'When he was setting his traps,' said Hop-along, 'he left his dog at home. I suppose he was afraid it would get caught in them. So we might hide in a field of thistles, or a clump of nettles. He would never look in there in case he got stung.'

'Sometimes we would hide in a clump of giant weeds down in the corner of one of the fields,' said She-la. 'He would never go in there either.'

'I wonder why?' mused Old Sage Brush.

She-la shrugged. 'I don't know. The ground down there is very soggy. Maybe he was afraid he would sink.'

'So the giant weeds might be another good place to hide

from this man,' said Bluebell.

Running Fox nodded. 'If we were too far from the black-thorns, we could run in there.'

'If he's putting down nets to catch us I don't think you should run in anywhere,' cautioned the old fox. 'Not even into the giant weeds.'

What the foxes were now talking about was giant hog-weed, a plant introduced over a hundred years ago by a man who had travelled to Eastern Europe in the time of Eng-land's Queen Victoria. From beyond the Black Sea, he had brought home seeds after seeing its huge flowers in the val-leys between the mountains. When the seeds germinated and blossomed in the walled gardens of the big houses, the plants were greatly admired for their extraordinary height and their flower heads which were as big as umbrellas. Nothing like them had ever been seen before and many people came to see them. But if the wealthy thought they could keep the giant flowers to themselves, they were greatly mistaken. It wasn't long before the seeds were caught by the wind. No walled garden could keep them in and they quickly sprouted as giant weeds along river banks and streams, disused land and damp corners of fields such as the one described by She-la.

'The trapper must have seen us going into the weeds,' said Hop-along, 'but he never followed us.'

'And did he never leave a trap for you in there?' asked

Running Fox.

'Not inside, but sometimes he would set the snapping jaws on the other side where we would come out.'

'If the man from the fur farm followed one of us in,' Black Tip suggested, 'he might step on the snapping jaws.'

'I told you,' said Hop-along. 'The trapper walks the fields no more. All his traps are gone.'

'I wonder why he was afraid to go in after you?' asked the old fox.

'I don't know. We never saw anything in there that frightened us. But there must be something.'

'Do you think the man from the fur farm knows what it is?' asked Bluebell.

'I doubt it,' said Running Fox. 'He may know a lot about foxes in cages, but from what I've seen of him he knows little about the likes of us who live in the wild.'

'He doesn't know the fields very well,' She-la confirmed. 'I've heard him climb through a hedge when there was a place farther down where he could have walked around it.'

'Maybe then,' Old Sage Brush said, 'we should do what Black Tip suggests.'

'You mean, get him to follow us into the weeds?' said Vickey.

'Why not? If he's silly enough to climb through a hedge when he can walk around it, he may be silly enough to walk into the weeds when he can go around them.'

'But what's the point in getting him to go in?' asked Black Tip. 'I mean, if there's no trap there for him to step on.'

'From what Hop-along tells us,' said the old fox, 'there's some other reason why he should fear to go in. If so, I think we should let him find out what it is.'

* * *

As they believed it was Bluebell the man was after, it was left to her and Running Fox to lure him into the clump of weeds. They waited until the others reported that he was close by, then crossed the field at a trot, taking their time so that he would see them. After all she had heard about what might be in the weeds, Bluebell was fearful of going into them, but was reassured when Running Fox went in first. Looking up, she saw that the giant flower heads almost obscured the sky as they spread out to catch the sun and she wondered what it was that the trapper had been afraid of.

By the time the two of them emerged on the other side, Bluebell had lost her fear of the giant weeds, but the fear of being captured by the fur farmer soon returned. During the next day or two they went into the weeds several times, just to make sure he saw them, and while Bluebell couldn't see him she could feel his eyes watching them. But then as Old Sage Brush pointed out, that was what they wanted.

Shortly after that, it was they who watched the man from the fur farm. They saw him kneel to examine the ground where he had seen the blue fox enter the clump of weeds, then try to walk around them. However, he quickly changed his mind for they saw him walking back, his hands held high as, with great difficulty, he pulled one foot after the other out of the swampy ground. He was obviously very hot from his exertions, for he then rolled up his shirt sleeves and paused to consider his options.

'What's he doing now?' asked Old Sage Brush.

'He's bending down again, looking in under the weeds,' Black Tip told him.

'He's taken a net from his bag,' Vickey added. 'I think he's going to go in under them.'

'Yes, he's gone in,' She-la said. 'He's probably going to put it in the middle of them, or on the far side.'

Bluebell smiled, saying, 'Now we'll see what happens.'

Inside the clump of giant hogweed, the fur farmer pushed aside the tall hairy stalks with his bare arms. The large leaves brushed against his face and he cast them aside with his hands. Kneeling, he started to string his net across the path where the foxes were sure to go. But before he could anchor it, his hands, arms and face began to itch. It was then he realised his mistake, but it was too late. Like those who had gone to admire the giant flowers in the walled gardens of the wealthy, he discovered that the fine hairs on the stalks and leaves exuded a toxic sap that burned the skin. And when he ran out into the sunlight, it burned even more.

From their hiding place, the foxes saw the man rubbing his arms and face, but they weren't prepared for what happened next. As the sap burned deeper into his skin, he ran up the field frantically rubbing his arms as he went. However, the rubbing made the itching worse. In his panic he crashed through the nearest hedge and his arms were scratched by the thorns. He started to scream and they could still hear him screaming as he ran away through the fields on the other side.

'He's gone,' Black Tip told Old Sage Brush, 'and somehow I don't think he'll be back.'

'I hope not,' said Bluebell. 'He deserved everything he got.'

Old Sage Brush smiled. 'Maybe he's discovered there are more to foxes than their colour.'

The foxes knew the man from the fur farm had been stung by the giant weeds, but they had no idea just how deeply. The severe itching and burning was only the beginning. While most of the foxes he had caged had died, he would live. But he would suffer horrible blistering, followed by scarring that would torment him for years. No longer would he breed foxes for their colour. Nor would he ever again torment the foxes who lived in Glensinna.

★ ★ ★

Old Sage Brush lay in the evening sun listening as some of the others told several younger foxes about their epic journey to the Hills of the Long Low Cloud. When eventually, the younger foxes left, he got up and made his way back to his earth.

'Have you noticed how grey he has become?' asked Vickey.

Black Tip nodded. Like his mate, he had noticed that the white fur on the old fox's chest had begun to merge with a greyness that was spreading over other parts of his coat.

'I don't know how he did it,' Vickey added. 'The journey must have taken a lot out of him.'

'It's what he wanted to do,' said Black Tip. 'He knew Bluebell and her friends wouldn't survive unless we showed them how. Come on.'

As the two of them disappeared over the edge of the quarry to return to their den, Running Fox and Bluebell watched the younger foxes sporting themselves among the weeds. They were almost fully grown and would soon be leaving to make their own way in life. What the future held for them, no one knew. But Bluebell had now put the fear of the fur farmer behind her and was beginning to think of her own future.

'I wonder what colour our cubs will be?' she said. 'I mean, whenever we have cubs.'

'Probably red after me,' Running Fox replied.

'Or blue after me!'

Running Fox smiled. 'Or maybe a little of both.'

Bluebell returned his smile and nodded. It was a thought

that pleased her greatly and she wondered how many cubs she would have. Maybe two – maybe even four.

In any event, she would tell them they were in the Land of Sinna and that the Great White Fox would watch over them – whatever their colour.

Author's Note

The breeding of animals for their fur – a practice called fur farming – is still allowed in the Republic of Ireland even though it has been banned in several other countries, including the United Kingdom which, of course, includes Northern Ireland.

In 2015 there were three mink farms in the republic, according to the then Minister for Agriculture, Food and the Marine, Simon Coveney whose department issues the licences. He told the Dáil that a group he had set up to review the industry had recommended that fur farming should be allowed to continue under licence and, on foot of its recommendations, his department had introduced more rigorous controls on licence holders in the areas of animal welfare, animal accommodation, security and nutrient management.

The Minister said it was not the practice to divulge the names and addresses of fur farms as this might prejudice the security of the operators' premises and the mink they kept. In this regard, he may have been mindful of an incident that occurred in 2010 when animal rights activists used wire cutters to enter a fur farm in Co. Donegal and free up to five thousand mink from their cages.

Licences from the Department of Agriculture are required for mink farms, and when I asked the department if a licence was required for breeding foxes for their fur, I was told: 'We are not aware of any fox farms in Ireland so licensing is not an issue.' The review group recommended that all fur farming should be subject to licence and it remains to be seen if that will be the case.

While some people prefer to wear imitation fur, or 'faux fur' as it's called, there are reports that real fur is making a comeback. In March 2014 a British newspaper carried a headline saying, 'Animal rights campaigners protest as fur comes back into fashion.' It added that 'millions of pelts will be sold for record prices this month as models wear fur on the catwalk again.' A year later the same newspaper reported that the fur trade was booming and was now a catwalk favourite. It said figures from the International Fur Federation showed that the industry was enjoying another year of considerable growth. The demand for mink, sable, fox and ferret had soared and farmers were stepping up production.

China, according to the report, remained one of the biggest producers of fox pelt, and together with Finland was responsible for 91 per cent of the 7.8m fox furs produced globally. On the British catwalks in 2014, it recalled, more than 60 per cent of shows featured fur, and at New York fashion week the figure topped 70 per cent. It added that while luxury labels had a long history of featuring real fur in their shows, fur was increasingly being used by newer brands as well.

The fur of the farmed foxes in my story, of course, has not ended up on the shoulders of a model as they have escaped. Together with the wild foxes, they seek safety in the shadow of the arching briar. This is a reference to two briars, the bramble and the wild rose. The unlikely decision of other trees to elect the bramble as their king can be found in the Old Testament. The parable in Judges 9:8–15 relates that after the olive, the fig and the vine had refused the honour, they asked the bramble to reign over them. The bramble replied, 'If in truth you anoint me king over you, then come and put your trust in my shadow.' The wild rose which grows to greater heights in our hedgerows may also have a lofty connection, as it is said to have inspired the simple five-petal design of the heraldic rose used in coats-of-arms in medieval Europe. Why it is also called the dog rose, isn't quite clear, but it is said that in days gone by its root was used to make a potion to treat the bites of rabid dogs.

Inspiration for the story in 'A Narrow Squeak' also comes from the Old Testament, which says a man of exceptional strength called Samson posed a riddle involving bees, honey and a lion. The riddle and the answer to it are told in Judges, 14:12–18. Incidentally, there's a story about foxes in 15:4–5.

Not a very nice one, as Samson uses three hundred of them to set fire to the corn of the Philistines. According to that story he ties the tails of each pair of foxes together and puts a firebrand 'in the midst between two tails'. It seems foxes were treated cruelly in those days too.

Man's cruelty was also responsible, at least in part, for Ratwiddle's condition, as we discover in *Run to Earth*, the second book in the series. The other foxes believe that because he is always hunting rats down by the lake, his brain has been addled by rats' urine or 'widdle'. Foxes, dogs and other animals can be infected by rats' urine. It is usually contracted through a cut in the skin and if people get it, it can be fatal. It is known as Weil's disease.

As Old Sage Brush and his friends travel towards the Hills of the Long Low Cloud, they find that man has inflicted even more pain on Ratwiddle. In *Run with the Wind*, the first book in the series, they journeyed north from Beech Paw, through Wicklow, Kildare and into Dublin. But where are the Hills of the Long Low Cloud? At one point the foxes wait for Brent geese to arrive, and this should give us a clue. Every year, Brent geese migrate from the Arctic region of Canada to feed on Ireland's coastal areas and grassy pastures farther inland. I imagine, therefore, that the foxes are travelling through Wicklow towards the east coast. But where exactly the Hills of the Long Low Cloud are is known only to the old fox, and he doesn't say!

Along the way, the foxes find refuge in a mound that has been the home of badgers for generations and is still occupied despite the periodic killing of its inhabitants. The Department of Agriculture confirms that the culling of badgers continues to be carried out in certain areas in the belief that they transmit TB to cattle. There has been very significant progress, it says, in bringing down the levels of bovine TB over the past five to six years as a result of a comprehensive range of measures 'not least of which is the badger removal programme'. It adds that the ultimate objective is to incorporate badger vaccination into the TB eradication programme. A number of trials are ongoing and 'targeted badger removals will continue in the medium term'.

The goats the foxes use to try and get at the honey in the beehives, are being kept so that the farmer can make cheese from their milk. However, according to a BBC television documentary I saw recently, goats have been bred for quite another purpose. I was aware that a gene from a luminous jelly fish could be put into a mouse to make it luminous. But in the United States scientists have gone one step further. The silk thread of spiders is among the strongest substances known to man, and the programme showed researchers on a farm belonging to Utah State University making more of it in an extraordinary way. They had transferred a gene from a spider to a goat. From the goat's milk they were able to extract spider silk, and expect one day it will be used by doctors to carry out repairs on the human body. Imagine!

I don't think there are any plans at the moment to get goats to produce honey. Thankfully that's still done by bees which, in the process of collecting pollen and nectar as food, pollinate our flowers and many of our crops, thus enabling them to grow and reproduce. Believe it or not, we have ninety-eight difference species of bee in Ireland, including the honey bee and twenty species of bumble bee. The remainder are species of solitary bee. However, it seems that a third of the species are threatened with extinction through starvation because they can't find enough wild flowers. That, the experts say, could have a serious effect on our own food supply.

To try and reverse this trend, sixty-eight governmental and other organisations have put in place an all-Ireland Pollinator Plan for the years 2015-2020. The idea is to allow more wild flowers to grow, rather than being eradicated, and to this end the organisers have enlisted the help of farmers, councils, road and rail companies, schools and gardeners, among others. Apart from farmland, obvious places where more flowers could be allowed to grow are roadsides and railway embankments. Most bees apparently prefer plants which have flowers at the blue, purple and pink end of the colour spectrum, while plants like clover and knapweed are particularly successful in attracting them. Apart from anything else, the flowers would bring a bit more colour to our countryside. Let's hope the plan works.

My late father kept bees and occasionally sold honey to supplement his meagre wage. I remember as a boy delivering honey to some houses but never realised there was so much to beekeeping until Clem Murphy of Paulstown, Co. Kilkenny shared his experience and his books with me and I would like to thank him for doing so.

We continue to have foxes in our garden, even though we live less than four miles from the centre of Dublin. Twice recently we had a visit from a grey squirrel. We also have magpies, one of which I photographed pecking the tail of a fox that was sitting in the garden watching the house. It illustrates just how daring the magpies are, but some years ago they met their match in our cat, Casper. He was lying on a white plastic garden chair and because he was also white, the magpies didn't see him. When they did, it was too late, at least for one of them. It was this incident that gave me an idea for the story involving Snowflake in 'The Trophy'.

When watching shooting stars, the foxes in my story see what they believe are the flashing tails of those who have gone to the afterlife. After the first three of my fox books – *Run with the Wind*, *Run to Earth* and *Run Swift, Run Free* – were translated into Japanese, Dr Neil Murray gave me a book called *The Fox and the Jewel* by Karen A. Smyers, which examines how the fox came to be associated with the worship of the god Inari in Japan. The author deals with various beliefs that were held in that part of the world and I was intrigued by references to white, winged foxes, spirit foxes that cross the boundary from their world to ours, even a belief in ancient China that there was a connection between the fox and meteors, probably because both have long tails.

Speaking of stars, I see the US Navy is reported as reinstating celestial navigation for recruits as a back-up measure because of concerns that computers used to chart courses with the aid of satellites could be hacked or malfunction. The foxes, it would seem, are not the only ones who are keeping an eye on the Plough, or as they call it, the Great Running Fox in the Sky to find their way at night!

One day when my granddaughter Annabelle was four, she saw vapour trails that planes had left on an otherwise clear blue sky. Turning to her mother, Samantha, she said, 'Look, Mammy, something has scratched it.' I was immediately reminded of the saying, 'Out of the mouths of babes', to which I might add, often come gems. It was such a lovely phrase that I decided to include it in my book, even though it is written for much older readers.

Tom McCaughren, 2016